SIMON JESSE'S JOURNEY

SIMON JESSE'S JOURNEY

Stan Dragland

A Groundwood Book
Douglas & McIntyre
Vancouver/Toronto

Douglas & McIntyre Ltd.
1615 Venables Street
Vancouver, British Columbia

Canadian Cataloguing in Publication Data

Dragland, Stan, 1942-
  Simon Jesse's journey

ISBN 0-88899-025-1

1. Title

PS8557.R33S55   jC813'.54   C83-098618-9
PZ7.D73Si

Cover art by Cliff Kearns
Design by Maher & Murtagh
Printed and bound in Canada by D.W. Friesen & Sons Ltd.

For Simon and Toby

Table of Contents

Part One

UNDERGROUND

I
The Plughole

Toads. Toad juice. Simon rippled his hands through the water. It was true that one or two of the toads had peed in his hands, but the bath was his mother's idea.

Simon sat in the plug end of the tub, facing the taps. Behind him Toby muttered a motor-sound for the plastic boat he was manoeuvring through the waves. Simon relaxed his grip on the rubber shark he held. The shark sank. Staring between his legs, at the white bottom of the tub, he took no notice. His mouth carefully, silently, formed a word: *toe-duh*.

In his mind, Simon watched Wayne Warner throw a toad as high as he could into the air, felt his stomach contract as the toad reached its highest point and, slow motion now, begin to drop. Down it came, and down, and Simon improved on what had actually happened then, by making Wayne catch it very gently and then cup his hands, one over and one under it. But the toad went up again, up, the flop in the stomach, the plummet . . . Simon wrenched his mind away from the afternoon, leaving the toad in mid-air, and made an effort to focus on the tub bottom. The plughole. But he didn't manage for long.

Now he was squatting with Toby in the back yard, near the Newton's fence, and they were letting their toads loose under the lilacs. One of Simon's toads was creeping into the lily-of-the-valley. For just an instant, Simon made his creeping toad glance back over its shoulder and begin to say thank you. But toads don't have shoulders, really, and they don't talk. And anyway how could they know they'd been rescued from Wayne Warner. From under the van up on blocks on the Warner's front lawn across the street. *It's nicer for them here,* Simon thought. *Nicer and a lot safer . . .* Without warning the toad he had left in the air hit the sidewalk with an ugly splat, as it had that afternoon, and Wayne's shout of laughter rang out again. Simon was suddenly on his knees, on his front, under the van, frantically gathering the other toads; then Toby was with him, helping; then they were watching the toads settle in where they'd be safe. Among the lily-of-the-valley below the lilacs towered over by the maple tree.

Toads are not like frogs. He'd said so to Toby, and Toby had disagreed: "They are so." Simon explained that he was thinking about the toad they'd seen creeping across a large rock at the cottage, and Toby knew what he meant then. They hadn't realized that a toad can sneak along very stealthily, moving each of its four feet one after the other. It gave them a new opinion of toads; they were no longer slow, fat, ugly frogs.

A brief squawk like a cork turning in a bottle neck recalled Simon to the tub. He blinked and looked curiously at the plug. Had it twisted a little while his eyes stared at it, while they'd actually been looking inward? *People don't say "plughole." They say "drain."* Or was the plughole just the beginning of the drain? Anyway, now Simon imagined his father singing his sad, funny plughole song, and silently sang along,

A mother was bathing her baby one night:
The youngest of ten and a tiny wee mite.
The mother was poor and the baby was thin,
Only a skellington

Simon paused at that, and grinned.

Only a skellington covered in skin
The mother turned round for the toad

Toad! Start again.

The mother turned round for the soap off the rack,
She was but a moment but, when she turned back,
The baby was gone and in anguish she cried,
Oh where is my baby? The angels replied:

Your baby has fell down the plughole;
Your baby is gone down the plug.
The poor little thing was so skinny and thin
He oughta been bathed in a jug.

Your baby is perfectly happy.
He won't need a bath any more.
Your baby has gone down the plughole–
Not lost, but gone before.

So he goes down, and he ends up: in Heaven. That skinny kid goes to Heaven. He dies and he goes up to Heaven. But what if . . . With a squawk of rubber against the sides of the drain, the plug again began to twist. And this time it kept turning, as Simon watched, and it lifted and popped out of the plughole.

A spiral spout formed in the water as it flowed into the drain. Simon watched so intently that the waterspout blurred and began to divide, and it seemed that the two little overlapping whirlpools, each with its dark, silver-circled centre, would soon slide apart entirely. And what would he see where the whirlpools had been? Because there was something just behind what he was looking at that he could almost . . . there was something like a memory he could nearly but not quite call up. He was concentrating so hard, though at the same time he felt completely relaxed, that he didn't feel the current begin to tug him, very gently, towards the drain. He closed his eyes, in case whatever was trying to form was not outside at all, but inside, so he didn't notice when he reached the edge of the whirlpool.

II

The Tower

Waist-deep in soapy water, spiralling round and down the inside of a tower at terrific speed–why wasn't he dizzy? Fast as he went, with the darkness growing into grey light, brighter all the time, he could easily see a plastic boat spinning in the stream across from him. He could almost reach out and touch a rubber shark. Then the water began to feel odd, less wet, and he was falling more slowly too. He looked down. He could see the centre he was spinning around getting larger and closer, as the water got thinner, and closer and closer, till

Thump!

"Ow!"

The stone floor Simon was suddenly dumped on was bone dry. The water that dumped him had not washed away; it had quit–disappeared–so all there was left to land on was his backside, not hard enough to hurt himself. His exclamation came from surprise rather than pain. Still, if he'd known the bump was coming he'd have thought twice about . . . What was he doing in that vortex of water anyhow? He looked around for the boat and the shark. They were gone. He looked back up the tower. Spiral stairs curled up and up and disappeared into darkness.

He stood up and looked around. He was in a small room, a sort of antechamber. The stones of the floor continued up the walls to eye-level (except in the tower, where they climbed up out of sight), then the natural rock took over. The place was part chamber, part cavern, and there were three openings that left it. He decided to inspect each one, but before he made any move there was a small whoosh! past his ear. He started violently and ducked and covered his head with his arms.

"Hi!"

Who said that? Simon looked up. He couldn't see anyone. And now there was another voice, but not out loud. Though it was deep and rich, the new voice did not fill the room. It welled up inside Simon and filled *him* with a tingling sort of apprehension–partly because it was so vibrant, but mainly because of what it said: "Simon Jesse." That was all, just once. Whose voice? Simon couldn't identify it, though he felt with a surge of excitement that he should almost be able to. Whoever had spoken knew his middle name.

"Listen, how are ya?" There was the squeaky voice again, and there was phht past one ear, then phht by the other. This time Simon didn't duck, and his eye caught a black blur emerging from behind his head.

"Hi there, anyway!" it said.

"Who's that?"

"It's me."

"Is it . . . Mr. Bat?" It looked like a bat, but it wouldn't stay still.

"That's right. Howsa boy?"

16

"Okay I guess."

"Well say now, that's great! That is dandy. Now look. They sent me ta show ya where ta go, okay? But fi-irst." He drew the word out dramatically and paused. *He sure is enthusiastic,* Simon thought. Aloud he said "Who's they?"

"Oho! He's sharp now, isn't he? That's fer me ta know and you ta find out," the bat said smugly. "First things first. So first . . . yer with me now, are ya?"

"Yes."

"Well first, ya see that ring in the floor?"

"Yes."

"Give it a pull. Gwan now."

Simon bent down and pulled at the ring. It didn't budge. "What's it supposed to do?" he asked.

"Try again," said the bat, "pull yer hardest."

So Simon pulled for all he was worth. Slowly the ring began to lift, and with it one of the flagstones in the floor. Seeing that, Simon let the stone subside, straddled it and gripped the ring with both hands. This time he pulled the stone up and aside in one motion. He got on his knees and looked into the hole it had been covering.

"Now whaddya see? There a package in there?"

"Looks like it."

"Well c'mon. Take it out, eh. Open it up."

The package was a fur bag, closed tightly at the top with a drawstring. Simon loosened the string and reached inside. There was something else made of fur in there, and also something hard. He dumped the contents out on the floor. A piece of bone with a curved horn sticking from it came rattling out first, followed by a fur suit in two pieces.

"So put it on," said the bat.

"What, the suit?"

"Yeah. Helmet too."

"Helmet." Simon looked at the bone thing again. He picked it up by the horn, then lifted it with both hands and lowered it onto his head. It settled down over his forehead and, a little lower, over the back of his head. It fit so exactly it might have been molded to him. He tapped it twice with his knuckle. *Hey! Decent!* He drew on the pants of the suit. The feet that were attached to them made Simon's own feet look like paws. There were no paws on the sleeves of the hooded jacket, though, so his hands would be free. He slid it over his head and it caught on the horn until he discovered by feel the hole made in the hood for the horn to slip through. Then he realized what the hood was for: it kept the helmet snugly on his head. Everything fit him perfectly. He'd been delivered onto the cool stone without a stitch on, and here was this suit that might have been specially made for him. Strange. He wished there was a mirror somewhere, so he could look at himself in his new outfit.

The bat had been flitting nervously about while Simon was dressing. "So," he said now, "let's move."

"Where to?"

"Right through here." To show what he meant, the bat whipped several times in and out of the opening on the right. Simon followed the bat, if you could call it following, because the fool thing kept swooping back and forth. He either couldn't or wouldn't stay in one place. It was hard listening to him talk, too, because he moved around so much and so fast. Simon discovered this when he asked about the other two entrances at the base of the tower. Why this passage rather than one of the others?

"Oh," said the bat, "nothin fer you in there, nothin fer you." He chattered away, fading in and out, so that Simon didn't gather very much from the fragments he heard. Something about a black king, or black kings in a row. For a hundred years? Something about a fight or a light in the dark? "No," the bat finished, "this's the passage ya want, Howard."

"My name is Simon."

"Well fair enough, Si. Call me G.H." As he said that, he streaked ahead and rounded a left-hand turn in the hallway. Simon heard him say something, then reappear in a flash. Only for a second. He disappeared twice more before Simon reached the turn. When he swung around the corner himself, distracted by the frantic flitting of his new acquaintance, he nearly walked right into a heavy iron grating.

Just on the other side of the bars sat a huge rodent with a horn in its forehead.

The portcullis was no barrier to G.H. "Well, here he is," he said, turning a couple of loops through the bars. "Now you hang loose, Si, and don't take none a them wooden watchamacallits." It was the longest intelligible sentence he'd uttered for some time. He sped off down the passage before Simon could say good-bye.

The new creature was looking at him through the bars.

III

Questions

Except to quiver now and then with what might have been excitement, the horned animal made no move. It simply stared, which made Simon uncomfortable. But then he realized that the creature was absorbed in its own thoughts, not looking at him so much as through him. He felt free to make his own inspection. *It's a rat,* he decided, but two things didn't fit: the creature was horned, and it was huge. If it rose from where it sat with its long tail curled on the floor, Simon judged that it would stand as tall as his waist. There was something disturbing about looking at it, something connected with the fact that Simon was also furred and horned, though he stood erect and he had no . . . he felt behind him. No tail, but there was a stub where a tail might have been. His movement seemed to remind the rat of his presence. Simon could tell he now had its attention. He cleared his throat, but got no response. Finally impatience got the better of him.

"Well?"

"Well?" said the other, sarcastically. "What's he mean, hang loose? He's always . . . he's always . . . ." The tone made it clear that anger had caused the quivering. The rat started again.

"What's a watchamacootie?"

"Don't know."

"'*Course* you don't know," the rat exploded. "Nonsense, that's all it is! I'll be sitting here, just as quiet as you please, and he'll flap out of nowhere with his 'Howsa boy, Howard?' Awrrr!" The growl was accompanied by thrusting motions with the horn, which made it clear what fate was being imagined for G.H.

Grumbling under his breath, the rat now arose and began laboriously to work a crank that lifted the portcullis. When he'd raised it less than a metre off the floor he stopped and looked expectantly at Simon. Simon looked back.

"Well, come under. That's high enough if you duck down." Simon ducked, thinking that he'd left better company than he'd joined, though "company" might not have been the best word to describe G.H.

"What's that for?" Simon asked about the barrier, which was dropping behind him.

"Some is not allowed past."

"Why not?"

"Too many questions. Now come along." Simon stood still. "Where to?" he asked, with an edge in his voice.

"I said let's go!" said the other, and he began to make his way down the corridor. Simon fought down an impulse to say something insulting. He hesitated, then began to follow. His annoyance left him as he walked, and curiosity took over. Questions tumbled through his mind. Where am I going? How come I'm expected? How do they know about me here? Is everybody here like this stupid . . . His guide scuttled ahead, glancing back impatiently now and then.

After the corner of the portcullis, the hallway continued straight ahead. Before long, they passed a heavy-looking door on one side of it. Then more doors, all of them alike, most of them closed. The thought of a dungeon alarmed Simon for a moment, and almost brought him to a standstill again. But he rejected the idea. The doors were rather pleasant to look at, their thick planks rounded at the top with the same curve he remembered in the arched corridor entrances back at the bottom of the tower. Each door had two large hinges, a handle, and a big bolt made of some unshiny black metal. As he passed the odd door that was ajar, he glanced in, but he had to move quickly to keep up, and anyway he didn't want to snoop. He did glimpse another furred creature through one door, and he heard quiet talk as he passed another.

There was no source of illumination in the hallway, at any rate none that Simon could locate; instead the stones themselves seemed to give off a slightly bluish glow. Fascinated by that, looking around, looking up, Simon started as he heard a small shriek and felt his foot pulled almost from under him. He skipped once to recover his balance, and lifted his foot to free the tail that was under it. The rat had momentarily panicked; his sudden release sent him scampering ahead to keep himself from tumbling. When he turned to glare at Simon, his tail curled protectively close to his body, it was clear that the incident had not improved his temper.

"Clumsy! Watch where you're stepping!" Simon said nothing; he was trying not to laugh, as the rat started off again, carrying his tail curled oddly to one side and with his hindquarters skewed a little sideways too, so that he scampered in a sort of dog-trot.

When he finally halted, it was in front of a door like any of the others. He glanced darkly at Simon and lowered his horn to knock.

Rap, rap. There was no response. Rap! Rap! Rap! Nothing. With a disgusted grunt, he horned the door open, stepped inside, and motioned Simon to follow.

As he entered the chamber, Simon once more heard the deep voice that had spoken back in the antechamber. "Simon Jesse," it said–a gentle roll of thunder.

"Shh." Simon stopped, immediately alert. "Did you hear that?"

"Hear what?"

"Someone said my name."

"Your name? Don't be silly."

Don't be a nitwit, Simon thought, as he watched the rat approach another horned creature who was sleeping on a low stone bench. *Someone knows my name, and someone wants to see me.* He couldn't have said how he knew.

The bench, curved all around the room, which was circular in shape and made of the same fitted stones Simon had seen in the hallway. On it the new creature slept soundly on its side, breathing deeply, head drawn in to the breast by front paws wrapped around the horn. A nudge of horn on the sleeper's back produced a spasm of stretching, a couple of hind-foot prances, a long, contented snore. A sharp poke in the rump had a more dramatic effect. The sleeper came awake with his feet churning the air and his body flinching in what seemed an effort to dodge imagined blows. Finally, with a violent twist, he reached his feet, where he stood in a crouch, eyes wild.

"You awake, Ben?" Simon's guide was unmoved by the effect he'd created.

"What? What?"

"If you're awake . . ."

"Arnold, by the Toad! Don't *do* that Arnold!"

"You got to move, Ben." Arnold jerked his horn in the direction of Simon, who was standing behind him, torn between anger and amusement at the scene he'd just witnessed. "The chamber is needed." Ben's indignation left him at once. His mouth dropped open and he stared.

"Is this . . ." he began.

"Let's *go*, Ben."

"Does Sarah know?"

"Leave it to me. You crawl in with Austin or Conrad for now. Now move!"

With one last look at Simon, Ben hurried out, leaving several more questions, some his, some Simon's, hanging in the air. But Simon was through talking to Arnold. Or so he thought until Arnold started for the door. Simon was on the verge of shouting Wait! when Arnold turned. "Wait here," he said.

"Wait for what?" But Arnold left without volunteering anything more. Simon supposed he ought to have expected that. The last thing he saw before the door closed was the sneer on Arnold's face. There was the harsh sound of a heavy click. Simon stood where he was for a moment, then went over to the door, half expecting to hear Arnold snarl at him from the other side. *Bolted*. Nothing to do but wait. Thoughts of dungeons came creeping back. Wait for what?

IV

Nightmare

He sat down on the stone bench where Ben had been sleeping and tried to piece together an explanation for what was happening. What was he doing here? G.H. seemed to have had some idea. Maybe if they'd been longer together, if he'd been able to slow the bat down . . . But Arnold. Simon realized that he felt about Arnold the way Arnold felt about G.H. His fists involuntarily clenched as he imagined his fingers encircling Arnold's neck. From behind, to stay clear of that horn. Choke some information out of him. But Arnold was gone. To tell Sarah, Simon supposed, whoever she was. Tell her what? He gave it up. Inside this locked room, the only thing to do was wait.

Except for its miserable occupant, the room was absolutely empty. There were no furnishings, nothing to examine that might distract him from the waiting. He tried counting the number of stones in the floor, kept losing track as his mind wandered. He got up and paced the room in contracting circles, counting as he walked. That would have worked, but he got bored with it. He tried avoiding the cracks, tried stepping always on cracks . . . Where *was* everybody? He was getting angry. He paused at the door and banged on it, first with his fists, then with his open hands. "Hey!" he shouted. "Hey! Anyone there?" All he got back was the muffled echo of his own voice, and it turned his anger into loneliness.

Feeling very sorry for himself, he sat down on the bench again, then stretched out on it. Not comfortable. He turned onto his side, put both hands under his head, drew his legs up almost to his chest. Tried the other side, same position. He wriggled on the rock till he found a slight depression to slide his hip into. Best he could do. He thought his way from the scene between Ben and Arnold back down the hallway he'd come through, to his meeting with Arnold, back around the corner with G.H. He remembered the pleasure he'd felt when he first put on his suit. That was gone now, though he was thankful for its warmth as he lay there. He remembered the sack he'd dumped it out of. *I could use that now, for a pillow*. He started to think his way back up the tower he'd washed down, and found that he couldn't. His thoughts, like the tower, darkened and petered out. He tried to blank his mind and then suddenly fill it up with the tower, hoping to surprise some evidence of where he'd come from. No luck. Tears welled up, rolling down his cheek, gathering in a pool behind a dam that was his nose. He wiped the pool away and closed his eyes.

When he opened them a moment later, it seemed that the mysterious light in the chamber had dimmed, and that imperceptibly it brightened again as he watched. But perhaps it was just him. He started to

27

experiment, closing his eyes and keeping them closed for various intervals, then snapping them open. Surely the longer he kept his eyes closed the weaker the light was. But his eyelids were also growing heavier. He never saw the room dim down to not quite pitch black.

In his dream there was no horizon where the land met the sky. The ground beneath his feet, if it was land (it was smooth as a floor, but there were no walls) was white. The sky was white. He was walking, though he couldn't feel his feet touch the ground. He looked ahead, only ahead, because he had the uncomfortable feeling that if he looked behind him everything would be black there. In fact the longer he walked the faster he wanted to walk, because the darkness at his back was hostile. But he couldn't move faster.

Then there was a speck ahead. He concentrated on the speck, on moving towards it. Hours seemed to pass before the speck grew into a ball, but then the ball began to grow quite quickly, though he seemed to be approaching it no faster. It changed as it grew, stretching upwards as though there were a smaller ball inside it wanting out. The shape of an egg. But it was a person, someone sitting in the white plain, someone with his back turned, dressed in white with his knees cradled in his arms and his head bent to his breast. Left, right, in painfully slow motion, he urged his legs forward. Years seemed to pass before he drew near enough to touch that huddled body on the back.

Something was wrong. Something was awfully

wrong, but he couldn't stop his arm lifting away from his side, lifting and reaching. Stop! he wanted to shout, and opened his mouth but there was no sound. The word stayed in his throat and the arm was lifting, extending, the index finger pointing . . .

At his touch (but he didn't feel the touch) a mosaic of cracks appeared all over the body in front of him. Then the head began to rise from the breast, began to turn, slowly, turn to look up at him, the back hardly budging, just the head, then the face . . . With a terrible sinking feeling, as though his insides were draining out, Simon realized what was wrong. He was looking into his own minutely cracked face. Then the face and the body, *his* body, crumbled. All the pieces fell in a heap on the plain and he saw that the body had been hollow. There was the dim impression of someone stealing away, just out of his line of vision, where the white plain met the black like two halves of a circle. Was it Arnold? Some charm was broken, anyway. The darkness flowed past him, overwhelming the light, while the plain beneath his feet began to stretch and curve till he was shaken to his knees, wrapped in a tube of night. The pieces of his own hollow body raining down, suddenly alive, insects. Frantically brushing them off . . . but suddenly the tube was shrinking, pressing on his shoulders. He lay flat, and still the tightening . . . He could hardly breathe, he opened his mouth and screamed with the last of his breath and this time he could hear the scream. Long and loud, and returning to him in a muffled echo . . .

"My goodness!" Simon heard as he struggled awake. "My *horn*, what a set of lungs!"

Two figures stood beside the rock bed. Raising himself on an elbow, Simon saw that one of them was Arnold. But the voice belonged to the other. Swinging his legs out and onto the floor, Simon rubbed his eyes and looked at her. She appeared somewhat alarmed but also curious and kindly. The expression encouraged Simon to speak.

"How long have I been here?"

That seemed to confuse her. "How long? Why, that's not so easy to say. But why do you . . ." A sharp gleam appeared in her eyes. "Arnold, you brought me here as soon as he arrived, didn't you?"

Arnold shook his head. "Finished my watch first."

"Arnold, you idiot! You wouldn't know your duty if it took a horn after you. In fact . . ." Simon knew exactly what she was thinking, and he thoroughly approved. Arnold backed away, sullenly. "Get out, Arnold," she snapped. "And tell whoever relieved you to lift the portcullis and leave it up." Still retreating, Arnold began to stammer an objection.

"Do what I say, Arnold! Get moving! Oh, and send Ben and Joe here."

Arnold took his sulk out the door. The newcomer, to whom Simon had taken quite a shine, watched him go, then turned. The anger faded from her eyes and her features relaxed into a friendly expression that also managed to convey apology.

"I'm Sarah," she said.

"I'm Simon."

"Simon," Sarah repeated, as though testing the

name, but with a satisfied tone that made it sound like the answer to a long-unanswered question. She made Simon sound like an excellent name, and its owner was now almost as relaxed as he had previously been tense. Here was someone likely to help him out of his bewilderment.

"Are you going to keep me here?"

"No. What did Arnold say to you?"

"He wouldn't tell me anything. He doesn't like me."

"I don't know about that. He probably likes you as well as he likes anyone. He has never been a winning sort, Arnold. But enough of him. You don't know what you're here for, then?"

"No."

"Well, then. You must have been wondering, to say the least. I'll have to do some explaining. Can you be patient just a little longer?" She touched his leg reassuringly with a paw and, when he nodded, turned to greet Ben, who now appeared with a companion, Joe.

So that the two would stop stealing glances at him and listen to her properly, Sarah introduced Simon, to whom they dipped their horns politely. When Sarah resumed her instructions, Simon listened closely. What he heard seemed to connect with some of the fragments of information he'd gathered from G.H., but nothing came clear, except that there was to be some sort of meeting.

"Joe, you're for the Midnight Lake tunnel. Don't forget what G.H. says about the creatures in the water. Stay well back from the edge and shout across to Humphrey on the island. Hurry now. It'll take them all some time to ferry across." Joe left the room at a run.

"Ben, The Row. Trot now!"

When they were alone, Sarah motioned Simon to sit down on the bench so that his eyes were more nearly on a level with hers. She looked at him searchingly, with an intensity that made him apprehensive about what was coming. She took a deep breath.

"Simon, I'll put it in a nutshell. You're here to lead the Horn People–that's us–you're here to lead us out of exile."

"I'm what!"

"I was afraid that might be a shock. Well, let me see . . . I'd better start at the beginning."

Part Two

UNDERGROUND

V

Sarah's Story

"A hundred years ago we lived in the sun. Well, we had our burrows in the side of a hill, but we spent most of our days in the open air. We rose with the sun and we retired with the sun. We still do. I guess the rhythm is in our blood, even down here, where nothing ever changes. I'm sure it was partly feeling the sun inside us that kept up our spirits and helped us to hope we'd get back to it some day. Of course we were also told to expect you. At least we'd been told to expect someone."

Simon had a strong urge to interrupt at this point, but his respect for the melancholy in Sarah's voice was even stronger. He could tell he was not listening to a casual tale; he was listening to Sarah's life. The telling had so quickly cast a sad spell that he could not bring himself to break it. It was what Sarah had suddenly sprung on him that now troubled him most—that he was expected to be some sort of leader. But he realized that Sarah was answering his questions in her own way, remembering a sad story that he was part of, somehow, or was going to be.

"Why did we lose the sun? That's hard to know. Sometimes I've thought the cause was just what was best about our life–the comfort, you know, and the regularity. We couldn't bring ourselves to believe that could change. We didn't believe it soon enough, anyway.

"What changed first was the earth, which had always been as much our friend as the sky was, and the sun. One night I woke up suddenly, frightened. Something had happened, and I wasn't sure what, but I found that everyone else in the burrow was awake too. Some thought they'd been dreaming that the earth had lurched or trembled or something, but we soon realized we wouldn't all have had the same dream. The trembling couldn't have lasted long, and it happened only once that night.

"In the morning we joined all the others outside, and that was when we really began to wonder. There was a rock formation near our burrows that we called The Giant–it was one big rock balanced on top of another. It had been there longer than anyone could remember, and now the top rock had toppled. *That* was no dream.

"We were talking things over when Arthur Toad showed up on the edge of the group, and someone asked him what he made of it all–half-jokingly, because no one took Arthur Toad seriously. Oh, there was a tradition, really a sort of rumour, that he had weird powers, but he kept to himself and no one had ever even heard him speak. So he was easy to ignore. But I'll never forget what he said that day. He said 'Earth has warned you once; she will not warn you twice. I tell you to flee this place. Earth disputes only with herself, but it is dangerous to overhear.' Those were his exact words.

"Well, he left us disturbed, I can tell you, and confused too. I mean, leave the place where we'd always lived? That was unthinkable to most of us. The only one who argued that we should leave without wasting time was The Row. Now I wish I'd listened to her. She has instincts. It's her job to have them, in a way. She's the head singer. But there it is–the easy life. There'd been no new songs for ages, only the old ones passed down from times before any of us were born, and we weren't listening to them the way we once had. So we didn't listen to The Row as we once would have, either. So what to do? Most were for staying. Some even said they'd be horned if they'd let a crazy toad drive them away from their homes. I couldn't bring myself to say we should go.

"The next two days and nights were quiet, but not long before morning of the third night we had our minds made up for us–too late. Say the earth had shrugged, the time before–something like that. This time it was as if she had a terrible fit of shaking and couldn't stop. It was terrifying. We didn't get out of the burrows much before they collapsed, I'd say, and then we didn't get far. The ground we were on was tearing in front of us and behind, and the patch we were on was sinking into it. I don't know how far it sank, but the last thing I saw before those new cliffs above us sort of leaned together was a bit of sky. The dawn was just beginning to light it up.

"It seemed to take ages, all this, but I suppose it

was no more than a few minutes till there we were, just lost. If I hadn't been too terrified to think, I'm sure I'd have thought it was the end of the world. The first voice I heard, out of the moaning and whimpering, was Humphrey's. You'll meet him later, him and The Row and the others. Humphrey was in a rage. He was cursing Arthur Toad, which I thought even then was kind of silly. Arthur Toad had tried to warn us, after all, but Humphrey seemed to think he'd somehow caused the whole thing. Well, Humphrey hadn't been going on too long before a small light appeared among us, and began to grow, and do you know what it was? It was Arthur Toad. His whole skin was glowing, very powerfully, though we could still look right at him without hurting our eyes.''

The door opened and Ben looked in. Sarah noticed him, but she didn't speak immediately. It was as if she had to recall her thoughts from a great distance. Ben waited politely.

"All right?" Sarah asked, finally.

"Yes, and Joe is back from Midnight Lake. What now?''

"Now spread the word here: a general council.''

Ben withdrew again. Sarah stood up and began to move towards the door. Simon could no longer hold back, now that the mood of the story had been interrupted.

"I don't understand, Sarah. What about me? How did you know about me? I mean why would it be me who . . . I mean, you're all more than a hundred years old, and . . .'' Simon's voice trailed off. Sarah didn't respond right away. When she began to speak again, it was almost as if to herself.

"Yes. Why you? And why us, for that matter. Don't think we haven't asked ourselves why we landed here, because it's not enough to know that we could have escaped. I've blamed and blamed myself for missing the chance, but I still can't for the life of me see that we deserved this." Sarah paused, reflectively, before resuming. "I've had a lot of time to think. I've had too much time. And the thing that's clearest to me is that there are more questions than there are answers. And you could get lost in some of the questions.

"But it was Arthur Toad who told us what we do know. He knew about this place, and he led us here. And he was the one who told us about you, though he wasn't very specific. A hundred years, he said, and then a deliverer would come. How he knows these things I could not say, and I expect he'd be the last to tell, assuming that he could. Maybe the oddest thing of all is that we're actually no older than we were when we arrived here. We don't seem to have aged at all. Now figure *that* out."

VI

Arthur Toad

Simon was not prepared for the transformation of the deserted hallway he had first entered with Arnold. Horn People were everywhere, rushing about, conversing excitedly. As he and Sarah stepped out of the chamber, a hush dropped over the crowd and all eyes swung to them. The Horn People stared at the boy in the fur suit. Then some of them unfroze and hurried down the hallway in the same direction that Sarah was taking with Simon; others slipped to one side to let them pass, some of them dipping their horns respectfully. Simon smiled and nodded, still giving most of his attention to Sarah, who continued her story as they walked.

Sarah strolled slowly, but she picked up the pace of her narrative, touching only the high points now, telling of the great difficulty of adjusting to life below ground, of the confusion of despair and anger, the squabbles and fights and the self-appointment of Humphrey as leader, supported by the most surly faction of Horn People.

"They found me easier to blame than Arthur Toad, and I guess that was understandable. I was in charge, after all, though it was ages since I'd had to decide anything important. And why make a big thing of your authority if there's no need. That wasn't Humphrey's approach, though. He proclaimed himself king, of all things, and began to impose what he called 'discipline.' It was just an excuse for bullying, though–all the rules he decreed and the strict routine he set up. Things got a lot worse than they needed to be.''

The buzz of excited conversation was growing ahead. Clearly they were nearing the meeting place. Soon they passed through an archway into a circular chamber not unlike the one they had left, except that it was huge. And instead of a single stone bench, there were tiers of them, so that the room was a kind of amphitheatre, rapidly filling up with Horn People. Sarah pointed out the well in the centre of the chamber, as she and Simon crossed the floor.

"That's Deep Well. That's where Humphrey found his 'crown.' " She spat the word.

"His crown?"

"Yes. So he called it, anyway. It was just a metal band, but he started to wear it on his horn, as though the silly thing raised him above the rest of us. He looked ridiculous wearing it, too. He might have realized that if he had any such a thing as a sense of humour.'' They were crossing towards an archway on the far side of the chamber.

"Isn't there going to be a meeting?"

"Yes, but first there's Arthur Toad to see."

Simon's stomach flopped, and he realized that it was full of butterflies. So much that was new to him– and now Arthur Toad.

"Well," Sarah continued, "to make a long story short, I finally had to step in before I lost all control. I tried to reason with Humphrey and his bunch, but they wouldn't have it. So there was a terrible fight. I gathered the others and we drove them right out of here, down the Midnight Lake tunnel and left them to cross to the Black Island there, where there's no light at all. The kingdom of the Black King–and he was welcome to it.

"It didn't hurt so much to get rid of Humphrey as it did to banish The Row and her singers. They didn't raise so much as a horn to help us. It wasn't in them to fight, they said, and I was so furious over the whole business I told them to clear out. They wandered down the Third Tunnel, and we dropped the portcullis and that was that. I've often had second thoughts about The Row. She's such a lovely harmless one, and it meant we've had no songs. I don't know. I *had* to take control. I kept their voice boxes too."

"The singers'?"

"Yes. Maybe that was wrong. Maybe it was too much, but . . ."

They walked in silence for a time, Simon with his hands behind his back, looking at the floor and turning the incredible story over in his mind. The buzz of the Council Chamber was steady behind them.

"The Row is an odd name."

"Well it's a nickname. Her given name is Janis, but no one has called her that since she became head singer. The name goes with the job, so to say, and it comes from a strange song that nobody knows where it . . . We don't know its origin. It's, uh . . . well I won't try to sing it, but the words are, let's see . . . Row row row your burp gently through the cream. Merrily merrily merrily merrily, something something steam. Hm.'' Sarah paused and cocked her head in a listening attitude, apparently running through the song silently, nodding to the rhythm. "No," she said, starting to move again, "I can't get that last bit.

"Ah," she said, stopping beside a low, circular door in the left side of the hallway. "Arthur Toad's chamber. If you can call it that. He dug himself in here. Got us to fill it up with soil and dug himself in backwards. All he said before he did that was 'Bring the boy to me when he comes.' The amazing thing was, soon as that door closed the hallway began to glow, and we realized Arthur Toad was giving his power to the earth so we wouldn't have to live in the dark. Except for Black Island. His power doesn't cross water.

"Now. This door has been shut for a long time. Let's see."

She lifted the bolt out of the latch, raised it, drew the door towards her. It swung easily, creaking only a little at the hinges. When it stood wide open against the wall, it was as if there were two doors, one the mirror image of the other but made of soil. Sarah spoke almost in a whisper now.

"This will be your job, Simon. Start scraping away that soil. Gently, now."

There was nothing but earth, crumbling easily and falling to the floor, for several centimetres. Then, in the exact centre of the circle marked by the doorway, Simon touched something that wasn't soil. The moment he did, there was a deep grumbling sound. The light in the hallway flickered off, then on. Simon leapt back.

"No, that's his nose. Nothing to worry about. Go ahead."

Gradually, very gingerly, Simon freed a beautiful big Toad's head from the soil. The eyes were closed. When the head was completely clear down to where it joined the body, Sarah said "That'll do." Then she addressed the head, and Simon noticed the tremor in her voice.

"Arthur Toad."

Instantly the eyes flicked open. They glowed with a greenish-yellow light. Then, though the mouth remained closed, there came that deep, friendly voice, the one Simon had first heard in the tower.

"Simon Jesse."

That voice! Simon recognized it with more pleasure than surprise. That it should belong to Arthur Toad seemed only natural, given all that Sarah had said about him.

"Yes, Mr. Toad."

"Arthur Toad!" came the sharp reply. Simon quickly corrected himself, and the voice sounded again, its resonant warmth restored.

"Sarah has spoken to you?"

"Yes."

"Sarah."

"Arthur Toad?"

"Your preparations?"

"Almost complete, Arthur Toad."

"Good. Now leave me with Simon Jesse." Sarah withdrew in the direction of the Council Chamber. Before she disappeared, Arthur Toad continued.

"Sarah will have told you why you are here. Can you recall how you got here, where you came from?"

"No, Arthur Toad. The first thing I remember is being in the tower, and . . ."

"Good," the booming voice interrupted. "For now you belong to us, even your memory. No distractions. You must concentrate on the job at hand."

Simon felt his heart sink. Sarah had talked about his leadership as though she took it for granted and, if Simon had not exactly shared that opinion, he'd had little oppportunity to consider what it might involve. Now the weight of it came crashing home.

"Excuse me, Arthur Toad."

"What is it, Simon Jesse?"

"Are you sure you have the right person? See, I've never . . ."

"You have no experience, and you are not old enough," Arthur Toad interrupted. His voice seemed to have little sympathy in it. "Listen, Simon Jesse," it continued, "I know what I know. The task is meant for you. There will be danger. I will not hide the fact. You will meet the danger and you will be stronger than your fear. You will do what you have to do. I know this. Simon Jesse, The Row and her singers will be singing your deeds as long as they live, and their songs will pass to their children and their children's children." Perhaps Arthur Toad wanted to encourage Simon with this matter-of-fact statement of a reward to come, but it merely confused him. It was beyond his power to imagine himself doing "deeds" at all, let alone deeds that would make anyone want to sing. Arthur Toad had to break the silence.

"They'll be singing your deeds so they can remember you and all you did for them. Now, you are needed at the Council Chamber. When everything has been settled there, you will return to me."

VII

Song of Silence

Sarah met Simon at the entrance to the Council Chamber and led him to the middle of the room, where he felt uncomfortably the focus of attention. Sarah drank briefly from Deep Well. "Help yourself," she said. Simon cupped his hands and drank, feeling the water cool its way down inside him. Refreshing. Then, as Sarah had sat down, he did too, on the edge of the well. Sarah had fallen silent, and the talk from the tiers died out as well. Two more Horn People hurried in and took their places. Everyone sat quietly in the gathering tension, watching the entrance. There was an air of expectancy in the room, and it wasn't long before Simon found out why.

Without any warning, a tall, thin creature entered the chamber. She had a very dignified if somewhat preoccupied air about her, and the expression on her face was melancholy. "The Row," Sarah announced quietly, though Simon could have gathered that from the whispers passing through the tiers. The Row was followed by fifteen others, most of whom looked as sad as she. When all of The Row's people were present, standing in a semicircle facing the well, Sarah began.

"Don't be glum, The Row. This is not a time to be glum, when our exile is so close to being over. This is a great day for us all."

For answer, The Row simply opened her mouth.

"Of course!" Sarah said. "Well, we'll soon change that. Mark, will you and Peter bring in that box?" Two burly individuals left and soon returned, pushing a chest made of dull black metal which scraped and rumbled across the floor. They left it in front of Sarah. The Row and her voiceless followers were all eyes, as Sarah horned up the lid, releasing a deafening rush of noise, a confusion of chatter, screams, laughter, moans, snatches of song. She dropped the lid and the room was quiet again.

"Would you listen to that!" she said to no one in particular. "That's your voice boxes without any brains attached. Now, people, get ready, because it's going to be something in here till we get all these voices delivered." Up went the lid again, and out came the madhouse noise. It completely shattered the tension in the room. Simon had to force himself not to laugh out loud, since there was no amusement on the faces of The Row and her people, as one by one they stepped up to receive a voice box. Each one given out was like a door shutting, and the noise was that much less. The Row was last, and then all was quiet until she began to speak.

"Sa . . . S. . . uh . . . a . . ." She cleared her throat. "Sarah," she finally managed. Then, "This isn't my voice. Who's got my voice?" She went around the semicircle of singers, listening to each, until she heard what she was after. "You wouldn't have gotten away with it, Horace," she said. "There's no mistaking this voice."

"Be fair," Horace replied. "I didn't have a chance to try it."

"Oh." The Row considered that. "True enough, Horace. Well, who else has the wrong voice?" The singers spoke up, testing, and there was a general exchange. When that was over, The Row seemed to remember the nature of the occasion.

"Sarah," she said, "it has been a sad, sad hundred years, because we couldn't talk to each other. Worst of all, we couldn't sing, and we were born to sing. To sing, Sarah, not to fight. I'm afraid we would refuse again. I must tell you that, because it was all that kept our spirits alive all this time, believing that we acted as we had to. But now that I've said so, I want to say that we bear you no ill will. You also did what you thought necessary. We know that. So." She approached Sarah, and the two of them crossed horns, on one side then on the other. Then The Row stepped back into the semicircle.

Slowly the singers spread out, side-stepping until they completely circled the well. When they were in position, The Row began to hum a single note, a lovely, mellow ribbon of sound that gradually took on a pulse and then a pattern of sombre melody. The other singers took up the rhythm first with their bodies, swaying from side to side. Then one by one they all raised their voices, humming every second phrase in mournful answer to The Row.

Ahh-ah

(ah-ah-ah-ah)
Ahh-ah
(ah-ah-ah)

Soon the Horn People on the tiers were swaying too, as were Simon and Sarah at Deep Well. The sound was soaked with sadness. Simon looked at Sarah through misted eyes. She leaned towards him and whispered, "It's a song of their silence. That's why there are no words."

Ahh-ah
(ah-ah-ah-ah)
Ahh-ah
(ah-ah-ah)

No words were needed to summon up a picture in Simon's mind, one that was there some moments before he remembered where he'd seen it: himself, sitting in a perfectly flat white plain with his back bent and his head in his arms–no other people or buildings, not a shrub, not so much as a blade of grass.

While the song lasted, everyone in the large room was absorbed by its lovely grief. When it stopped, the sadness carried on into the silence. The singers stood in their places for a moment, then The Row led them up to join the others in the tiers. As they filed off, the rest of the Horn People started a low chant, patting time on the stones with their paws: "Row Row Row Row." The chant was low and quiet at first, then it picked up speed and volume until, by the time all the singers had taken their places, it filled the chamber: "Row! Row! Row! Row!" Deeply moved by the scene he had just witnessed, Simon too chanted his joy at the reunion. But he stopped abruptly when he happened to glance at the entrance and saw there one whose glowering into the room made it clear what he thought of the celebration. The crown was still on his horn. Simon knew he was looking at Humphrey–The Black King.

VIII

A Sword For A Crown

"Terrible" had been Sarah's description of the fight with Humphrey. Now that he was looking at her adversary, it came home to Simon what that meant. Humphrey radiated force. The crown, which looked as if it had been tossed onto his horn like a ring on a peg, was not funny–not to Simon. To him it looked disturbingly wrong, and it increased Humphrey's menace. For the first time, Simon felt glad of his own size. He was the only one in the chamber larger than The Black King.

Humphrey was in no hurry to enter. He waited, as the noise died down, until he had everyone's attention. Then he snarled something over his shoulder, stepped into the chamber, and stood aside while a string of followers marched into the room. Perhaps they had rehearsed this entrance; it did seem something of a performance. Humphrey's followers were not as impressive as their leader, but they were very well-disciplined. It was easy to see that even outnumbered two to one they would be a force to reckon with. Without any hesitation they split into straight rows–four rows of ten each–and sat in their places.

Humphrey sauntered to a position in front of his troops, facing Sarah. He directed a long look at Simon, beside her. If he was impressed, or even curious, he gave no sign of it. Then he turned his attention to Sarah.

"Well?" His tone reminded Simon of Arnold.

"Well yourself," Sarah replied mildly. "You know why we're here. What have you to say?"

"You must be joking, Sarah. Surely *you're* the one to speak." Clearly, he wasn't going to make things easy. Simon found himself bristling with a fierce loyalty to Sarah. The fierceness of it surprised him. Sarah hadn't taken long to win his affection. And now she captured his admiration, too, because she didn't rise in the least to Humphrey's provocation.

"Why yes," she said, "I do have something to say, though maybe it's not what you expect. It's this: you have a choice to make. I can't see it taking much thought, not unless you've forgotten what it's like to live in the sun. Because this is Simon" (nodding in his direction). "He's going to take us back there." Humphrey's eyes flicked to Simon once again, but he took no notice of the introduction, and Sarah continued. "It's only right that you should come with us, and we want it so. But it has to be clear that *I* speak for the Horn People, now and when we reach our destination. I will answer to one person only, and that is Simon."

Again the measuring glance. Followed by a long pause in which Humphrey stared fixedly at Sarah, and she at him. It was Humphrey's gaze that finally wavered. Whatever he may have been thinking, he was not fool enough to deny that Sarah had the upper hand.

"All right," he said. "I accept your conditions." There was an audible release of held breath from the tiers. But it was premature.

"Fine, Humphrey. Now give me your, ah, crown."

Humphrey had not been expecting this. He rose to his feet. The outrage on his face spoke before he did.

"Why?" It wasn't exactly a question; it was defiance.

Sarah's tone was as level as ever. "Give me the crown, Humphrey. You won't be needing it."

The atmosphere in the room was like an overinflated balloon. One more breath and it might break. Or else it would slacken and go limp as the air rushed out. *What if he won't give it up?* Simon rose, took one step forward, added his silent challenge to Sarah's.

"Humphrey?" she prompted. His thick body abruptly relaxed. He made no answer but to lower his head, so that his horn was parallel to the floor, the crown dangling on it. Sarah advanced, lowered her own horn and snagged the crown. In the same motion she turned back to Deep Well and flung the crown

54

into it. Humphrey's composure broke. He rushed to the well, perhaps in time to catch a glimpse of the metal ring, no longer a crown, sinking from sight. Simon didn't care for the look he threw at Sarah when it was gone. Perhaps Humphrey was the only holdout, because his group took their places on the tiers readily enough, but he was an ominous one.

The meeting seemed to be over, but Sarah made no move to announce the fact. Simon looked at her to see why. She had handled things beautifully so far. What was she waiting for now? Why was she looking at him? He had an uncomfortable moment before he heard the rich voice of Arthur Toad speak from inside him.

"Look into the well, Simon Jesse."

As soon as he did, the surface of the water that had swallowed the crown was broken again, this time by what appeared to be the hilt of a sword. "Pick it up." Simon pulled from the water a scabbard, very plain but made in beautifully clean lines of the familiar black metal, and attached to a belt. "Put it on." Simon strapped the belt around his waist. "Now, draw the sword." There was a gasp from the Horn People as the blade emerged, because it shone with an intense light.

Simon was as astonished as the rest. He looked with awe at the blade he held vertically in front of him. The glow made its edges seem indistinct, but when he tested the edge between thumb and forefinger it felt solid enough. And razor sharp. He almost cut himself when Sarah shouted.

"Simon Jesse!"

"Simon Jesse!" The name resounded back from the tiers, in one voice made of many. The Horn People were saluting their leader.

IX

Riddles

"This is the last time we will meet face to face, Simon Jesse, so listen carefully."

"Aren't you coming with us, Arthur Toad?"

"No. The way is not suited to legs like mine, and one as old as I am is well enough here. Listen to me now.

"First a word of warning about Humphrey. There is much of the Black King in him still."

"I saw that."

"Yes, he has not been a credit to his people, though you have not seen the whole of him yet. Just be careful. Either the Horn People follow you, or they do not find their way out. It is as simple as that.

"Now. The company will follow you to the tower. Opposite the archway that leads here there is a stone door cut into the rock. Perhaps you noticed it?"

Simon called an image of the antechamber into his mind, but saw no door in it. "No, I'm afraid not."

"Well, I doubt that it would stand out unless you were looking for it. In any case, behind that door is a tunnel. It will be dark, because my will does not reach into it. But you have your own source of light now. There will be a long trek through the tunnel, and the tunnels forking from it. Remember this clearly: you must always take the turning to the right, no matter how small or unused it may look. The Horn People will travel single file behind you, and they must all be careful to stay close to the one immediately ahead, or risk missing the way in the dark.''

"Arthur Toad, who made these passages and the tunnels and the doors and all?''

"They were made long ago by the Mole People. The Moles are great craftsmen. The stonework here is second to none. The Moles make things to last, even though they never stay long in one place themselves. They have been delving, century by century, into the centre of the earth. They are drawn by the centre of the earth, where the rock is so hot that it flows.''

"What then?''

Arthur Toad paused only briefly before changing the subject.

"Forget the Mole People, Simon Jesse. You have more important things to think of. What have you learned so far?''

"Always turn to the right and make sure that everyone stays together.''

"One more thing. There will be no need to rush, but you will not want to waste time. There are creatures living in more distant tunnels which connect with the ones on your path. It will be simpler if you do not meet them.''

"What, are they dangerous?''

"They can be. With any luck, though, you will not find out. And there is your sword, if you do. It is no ordinary sword. Its name is Lightning and the one who wields it in need is no ordinary swordsman.

"Now, what you have been told already will serve for much of the way. The rest I cannot make so plain. The rest . . . the . . ." Arthur Toad's voice was dwindling, changing. His eyes were deepening into green, through blue, to purple, dark and stony. Whatever he saw with them now seemed unlikely to be near, while the voice faded to an indistinct murmur before words began to form as out of a great distance, in a hypnotic, metallic monotone.

> mmm   nna   nn
> the tunnel   tightens
> the way out   is wooden
> drive it   to daylight
> below   the beast
> the footbridge   before
> the far side   is freedom
> is freedn   nnfree . . .

The words sank into the mumble they had come out of. Then silence fell, as Arthur Toad's eyes returned to their normal hue, and in dismay Simon tried to figure out what it was he'd heard. *A beast, a footbridge, What else? A wooden . . .*

". . . you return," Arthur Toad's normal voice broke in.

"Pardon?"

"You return alone. You are to go back up the tower you came from."

The tower. Already it seemed ages since he had arrived at the bottom of those steps.

"Where does the tower take me, Arthur Toad?"

"Up the tower you came from you will find your greatest strength. You will find your past and your future."

"Arthur Toad, *what* are you . . ." Simon stopped before he said something he might regret, but his patience was strained to the limit. Nobody had asked what *he* thought of this whole business, nobody had asked if he *wanted* to be leader. And then to be told riddles when he was expecting answers, instructions . . . What beast, anyway? And the creatures in the tunnel, and the Mole People. What was Arthur Toad hiding? Simon was close to tears.

"I know, Simon Jesse," Arthur Toad's voice soothed, "I know. I would have made it clearer if I could. But I have told you enough. I have told you everything, in fact. Trust me, and you will see. And Simon Jesse."

"Yes?"

"It is a poor leader who feels no fear."

What was there to say? Already he felt ashamed of doubting Arthur Toad. Sarah needed his help. They all did. That much he understood, and it was no small thing. He gathered himself to apologize, but Arthur Toad forestalled him.

"Never mind, Simon Jesse. It is time for you to leave. Place your head close to mine." Simon quickly looked up and down the hallway. Was there a need to whisper? He presented an ear to Arthur Toad's mouth. Immediately something sticky touched his cheek.

"Is that it, Arthur Toad?"

"Yes."

Simon straightened up. "What was it?"

"It was a kiss."

"Ah."

"Now close the door and be off. Sarah and the others are waiting. Fare well, Simon Jesse."

"Good-bye." Arthur Toad's eyes were closed already, and he was shrugging the soil into place around him. "Good-bye, Arthur Toad." A last look, then Simon closed the door, replacing the bolt in the latch. As he hurried towards the Council Chamber he found himself smiling.

X

Sharp Eyes

A weird wailing, punctuated with dull, rhythmical thuds floated down the corridor to meet him. The closer he got to the Council Chamber, the more piercing was the wail. Otherwise it was constant, while the thudding grew at once sharper and more hollow. Just before he passed through the archway, he realized what it must be: the clack of horn upon horn.

The Row was responsible for the astonishing wail. As he slipped into the chamber, Simon remembered the first words he'd heard from Sarah: "What a pair of lungs!" The noise could hardly have been more surprising, coming as it did from the singer of the melancholy lament at the meeting earlier. Pairs of Horn People, standing head to head on the tiers, or spread out on the floor, beat time with their horns. The rhythm caught Simon up as he stood at the rim of the room, unconsciously shifting from foot to foot with it, and thrilling when, every so often, The Row burst into a fierce descending yodel and the Horn People responded with wild howls and yelps.

Some were not taking part, and Simon was worried that they might be Humphrey's people until he noticed Sarah among them, and Ben, and then picked out Humphrey performing with the rest. He considered sidling over to Sarah to ask what was happening and why she wasn't doing it, but then he saw her howl with the others and realized she was very much involved, even if not with her horn. Now was clearly not a time for questions. And anyway, the ritual was drawing him in, as on and on it went, with no new variation except for an almost imperceptible acceleration of rhythm that built and built until his body felt as though it were filling up with sound. And then after a prolonged, ragged howling that gave him the shivers, it stopped.

His body still tense and his mind clear, Simon came out of the spell to find Sarah beside him. He followed automatically as she moved towards Deep Well, and felt no panic when he heard her say that he was to tell the Horn People what he wanted them to do. He turned to face them before nervousness could catch up with him, and drew Lightning. As before, all eyes swung to the glow.

"People of the Horn," he began, borrowing something of his style from Arthur Toad, "I belong to you. Arthur Toad says so, and he says that you must follow me. And Arthur Toad knows." (*Much better than I do,* he thought, but that was not a thing to say aloud.) He was encouraged to hear a murmur of agreement. "We have to pass through some dark tunnels. My light" (he brandished Lightning) "will show the way ahead, but you will be behind me, in single file. Single file, because there are branches in the tunnels and you have to keep together.'' He paused to replace Lightning in the scabbard, and to give himself a moment's thought. What more could he tell them? Nothing, he decided. Nothing that wouldn't confuse and perhaps frighten them. ''That's all,'' he finished, knowing it wasn't. He didn't know what caused the stab of loneliness he felt.

''Sarah, is everyone ready?''

''Ready, Simon.''

''Let's go then.''

Sarah was beside him when he reached the hallway. ''That was fine, Simon,'' she said quietly, before the others caught up. ''Just fine.'' Actually, he thought so himself, though he was too preoccupied with the task ahead to stand back and admire the figure he was cutting. But he was glad to feel Sarah's support.

''Does it matter what order we go in?'' she asked.

''I don't think so. Whatever you think best.''

''I'll see to it, then.'' And she dropped back.

He passed the empty chambers off the corridor, all the doors standing open. He passed the raised portcullis, turned the corner, reached the antechamber. There was the fur bag, still on the floor. He nudged it to one wall with his foot. No sign of G.H. Now, what about the stone door?

There didn't seem to be a stone door. He had to

stop the Horn People from spreading out into the antechamber and filling it up, sending the word to halt back down the line. Then he approached the wall for a closer look. Yes, there did appear to be a seam in the rock that might outline a door. But no handle. He tried pushing first at one side, then the other. Nothing. He was conscious of Horn People surrounding him, watching. A youthful voice piped up.

"Are you looking for a pull?" Simon recognized Joe, one of the messengers Sarah had sent to spread the word of his arrival.

"Yes I am."

Joe reared onto his hind legs and scratched with his front paws at a section of the rock near the right side of the seam. It depressed at his touch, and Simon saw what he was looking for. "Right," he said, relieved, and Joe withdrew. Simon probed the area with a finger till he found the pivot point of a rock ring set so cleverly into the wall that he could easily have missed it.

"Those are sharp eyes, Joe," he said with gratitude, and was pleased to see the sharp eyes shine with pride. "Stand back now." Joe and the others crowded away. Simon grasped the ring with two hands, braced himself, and pulled. The door swung heavily but silently open, releasing a draught of cool air into the antechamber. Simon looked briefly into the dark tunnel behind it, then turned to give the signal to move. The lower steps of the tower caught his eye.

"Where you came from." Yes, *but first things first.* He drew Lightning, pointed it into the darkness. *Here goes.*

There was a slight commotion behind him before he'd taken two steps into the tunnel. He looked back, startled, but it was only Joe, scuffling to be second in line.

They were under way.

Part Three

THE JOURNEY

XI

Tracks and a Test

The Horn People walked almost soundlessly, as a rule, as did Simon with his feet encased in fur. But whatever sound their shuffling might have made, in the first reaches of the tunnel, was muffled by a fine grey dust that covered the floor to a depth of three or four centimetres. Each of Simon's footfalls made a small, smoke-like puff. The slight cushion of dust was pleasant to the feet, but it was not so agreeable to the nostrils of those farther back. Not that Simon understood the reason for the coughing behind him until he heard Sarah calling and hurried back to her. The farther down the line he went, the thicker the air became, until Lightning could scarcely penetrate it. He almost passed Sarah in the gloom.

"Simon!"

"Oh, Sarah. This is bad, isn't it." Even with his free hand shielding his nose and mouth as best it could, he was inhaling dust. He could feel it gathering on his face.

"I think we'd better stop until it settles a little," Sarah said. "Then we'll have to try to pick our feet up more."

"Right." Simon made for the end of the line. His

eyes were narrowed to slits, but they watered so much he almost had to feel his way. He sensed, more than saw, that he'd reached the last of the Horn People. "Hello?" he said. Several voices responded, and he recognized The Row's among them. "We'll rest until this settles," he said, then asked her to send word forward when the air had cleared. Almost choking now, he rushed back, holding his breath from about half way, and releasing it with a whoosh when Joe came into view. The Horn People were obviously managing better than he could, or there might have been some panic back there. But the pause was necessary. He sat down beside Joe, resting his back against the tunnel wall, rubbing at the teary grit on his face.

"Phew!"

"You're covered with dust," Joe observed.

"I guess so." Simon brushed at his chest and legs, without much effect. "It's thick back there."

"Joe," he said, after a moment's thought, "some of you weren't, you know, using your horns back at the Council Chamber a while ago."

"No, it's their Time."

"Time for what?"

Joe glanced up at Simon's own horn before he answered. "Horn Time," he said, "when we get our new growth, but it doesn't happen to everyone at once."

"But I thought Sarah said you haven't grown down here. At least she said you haven't aged."

"I . . . guess not. I haven't thought much about it. But we've all had our Horn Times anyway. Sarah made a mark on the wall of the Council Chamber for every one of hers, so we knew . . ."

Simon was distracted by a buzz passing up the line. It grew into the message he'd been waiting for. He rose to one knee. "Sorry, Joe. What were you saying?"

"We knew just about when you'd be coming. By the marks on the wall."

One of the others, who had been listening, spoke up. "There were ninety-nine of them."

So that was how the Horn People kept track of time without a sun to count the days by. It hadn't even occurred to him to wonder.

He moved more carefully now, but it was impossible to avoid raising a certain amount of dust, and the group had gone little farther than before when the request came up for another pause. This time Simon didn't sit it out with the others. He ventured a little way down the tunnel to investigate some marks on the floor he could see from where they'd stopped. *What's this*, he wondered, approaching them. *Tracks*? He looked back at his own trail, and noticed he had not been lifting his feet as high as he'd thought. But there was no resemblance between the tracks he'd left and those he was looking at. Not that the marks were easy to read. It looked as if something had come this far, then turned and gone back over its own trail. Whatever it was seemed to have, not paws, but something sharp for feet, by the look of those narrow, wide-set scrapes in the dust. It wasn't possible to imagine a creature to fit them, but their existence was alarming enough. He returned to the head of the line with the message to move. The dust should almost have settled, anyway, but he didn't feel like waiting longer.

Dust soon ceased to be a problem. First it was not so thick, then it disappeared entirely, as if it had been blown into the end of the tunnel by some underground wind. Now he was moving over rock, not perfectly flat or regular, but smooth to the touch as though polished by water, or by many, many feet. Mole People? Perhaps. He could see no scratches, anyway. He hoped that was a sign that whatever had left the tracks back there was not in the habit of coming this way.

The dust had been a nuisance, and the tracks in it an unpleasant puzzle, but the tunnels branched every so often, as expected. Simon bore always to the right, satisfied enough with the progress made so far, though he knew instinctively that the hardest part was yet to come.

Now he reached a triple fork. The middle way was much the largest of the three. The sound of running water, apparently not far into it, was very tempting. But he scarcely hesitated before leading the Horn People into the smaller passage on the right, treating his imagination to a drink. It cleared none of the dust from his throat.

Dryer than ever, he was some way down the most recent fork when the sound of angry voices erupted behind him. He turned and headed for the disturbance on the run, rather unnecessarily calling the order to stop over his shoulder.

What now?

By the time he reached it, the argument was a fight. He recognized only one of the two struggling Horn People by his powerful back. Humphrey had someone pinned, so that only a pair of hind feet were visible underneath him, frantically thrashing at his sides. The two were at such close quarters that there was no chance for horning, but Humphrey was using the advantage his weight gave him to go for the throat.

"Stop that!" Simon grabbed a handful of fur at Humphrey's neck. He pulled as hard as he could, but had to let go when Humphrey jerked his head up violently, narrowly missing Simon with his horn. So Simon gave him the flat side of Lightning. And again, as hard as he could slap. Was he going to have to use the point? But the next slap must have found a soft spot. Humphrey rolled away and scrambled to his feet. Only the levelled blade of Lightning kept him from launching himself at Simon, whose eyes never left the threat, though he was aware of Sarah now getting to her feet.

"Sarah! Are you . . ."

Humphrey was at bay, but he still had his voice. "Leader!" he snarled. "Where are you taking us? You passed the right way. Anybody could . . ."

"Shut up, Humphrey!"

"Anybody could tell that we took the wrong tunnel back there."

"Humphrey, I said hold your tongue!" Simon made as if to thrust with Lightning, and Humphrey flinched back into a crouch.

"I'm all right, Simon," said Sarah, to his great relief.

"Are you sure?"

"Nothing serious. Humphrey doesn't care for the route."

"I gathered that." He had also gathered something else: it was time for him to deal with the former Black King, and he was in the mood for it, after the violence done to Sarah, the needless delay.

"Humphrey, you're a fool. Didn't I tell you where my orders come from? And don't you have some reason to believe Arthur Toad? Do you want us to lose our way?"

"Listen, Simon Jesse," Humphrey hissed, "I've had my time in the dark or I might have been fooled back there. I tell you that middle tunnel is the one!"

Simon had heard something of Sarah's poor success with the reasonable approach to Humphrey, and he could see how useless it was now. So he simply turned Humphrey's words back at him.

"Fine, Humphrey. You take the middle tunnel, then. Take it by yourself. Go on. You're wasting our time."

Humphrey could have read his defeat on the faces of the Horn People around him. They might all have been too frightened, or too startled, to interfere with him before, but now they stared at him without sympathy. Humphrey was on the spot, and Sarah tried to help him off it. She spoke severely enough, but her tone was not unkind.

"Think, Humphrey. Use your thick head for once, and give it up."

Simon pressed his advantage. "This is your last chance, Humphrey. What are you going to do?" Of course there was no longer any question about that, but pride might have kept Humphrey's defiance up longer if Simon had not taken his silence as answer enough. "All right, move," he said, waving Lightning at the tunnel ahead. "I want you with me."

There was so little of the Black King left in Humphrey's step that Simon, following, felt a wave of sympathy, and of regret for what he'd had to do, almost as if Humphrey's defeat were his own. He had survived the first test of the leadership he had accepted at the Council Chamber, but it gave him no pleasure.

XII
Which Way?

There was no telling how large the cavern was, but it seemed immense, eerily swallowing the light before it could reach either ceiling or far wall. Simon stood peering into the darkness while the Horn People filed in and gathered around him for their first rest since Humphrey's revolt.

Simon had walked behind and a little to one side of Humphrey, to let Lightning show the way ahead. He'd thought a good deal about what it would take to reach Humphrey, how he might soften the humiliation of defeat. He was in charge of the Horn People only for as long as it took them to find their freedom, and perhaps it wasn't up to him to make peace between Humphrey and the rest. But Humphrey's isolation nagged at him–not so much because he wanted no more rebellion, though that was part of it. But he could see Humphrey becoming a permanent outsider, even above ground. A sad picture. What could he say that wouldn't be taken as a sign of weakness? Humphrey showed no weakness himself, unless it was between the ears. "You were right to come with us," Simon said finally. The only response was a grunt, which might have meant anything, so Simon dropped the matter. Neither of them had spoken the rest of the way to the cavern.

There was nothing to see beyond Lightning's reach, so Simon turned to watch the rest of the Horn People arrive. He was relieved to see Sarah move in as freely as the others, and was touched when The Row went directly to her and began to lick her wounds. Simon joined them and squatted to watch. "Nothing that won't heal," said Sarah cheerfully, and that seemed to be the case.

"Simon Jesse." It was Joe.

"Yes."

"Are we going back to where we lived before?" The quiet conversation near them died out. Joe was not the only curious one.

"Well, I don't know that," Simon replied, "but do you want to go back there? Wouldn't it be . . ."

The Row looked up from her work. "That's right," she put in, "there wouldn't be much left of it."

They thought that over in silence. Eventually Sarah laid the question to rest.

"We're going wherever we're going," she said. "Arthur Toad sent us this way, and that's good enough for me. We'll see where we're going when we get there." This was greeted with nods, and murmurs of agreement, and one of the listeners spoke for the others.

"I don't care. Anywhere will suit me fine, as long as it's in the sun." Everyone agreed with that, too. Simon smiled inwardly, but with admiration. Sarah certainly knew how to say the right thing at the right time, even if there wasn't much to it.

Now. He stood up. Between the mouth of the tunnel they'd come through and another very like it, first on the right, there was only a shadowed depression in the rock.

"Everyone ready?" A rustle of rising. Surprisingly, Humphrey moved to the tunnel without being told to, then into it when Simon said "Okay, let's go."

Something didn't feel right. Something was trying to slip into the corner of his mind's eye. He concentrated on letting it in. When it came, it was only that depression between the two tunnels. Nothing to worry about. But his steps slowed anyway, and he came to a halt, causing a chain reaction of collisions. Moving into the darkness, Humphrey cast an inquiring glance behind him. "Hold it a minute," Simon said. He was impatient to press on, and he felt sure that he was on the right track. Almost entirely sure. Still, it might be better to get rid of that "almost." "Back up, everyone," he sighed.

Some of the Horn People had not yet entered the tunnel. "What's wrong?" they asked, as he reached the cavern again, "What's the matter?"

"Nothing," he reassured, "just something I want to check."

The depression was below the level of his waist. He stooped and stabbed Lightning into it. There was no resistance, so he got down on his knees for a look. Then a cold sweat started up under his suit. There was a lip of rock overhanging the entrance to what was indeed a tunnel of sorts, making it appear from the outside much smaller than it actually was. But this tunnel was nothing like the ones he'd gotten used to. There wasn't even room to stand up in it. Was this hole large enough to count as the first turning? He hated to think so.

"Wait here," he said, and started to his right around the cavern wall. It wasn't long before he realized it was lucky he hadn't been drawn too deeply into the darkness, and the Horn People with him. It would have been easy to lose his bearings and confuse one entrance with another, because there were many of them, and very much alike. But there were other small ones too, some even entering the cavern well above his head. Perhaps three quarters of the way around it, with the Horn People still invisible across from him, he paused in front of one good-sized opening. He thought he'd heard something in it. A clicking noise? Quite distant, if it was. He didn't stay to make sure, but hurried to complete the circle. *The tunnel tightens.* Yes, but he'd expected it to happen gradually. He wished, desperately now, that he'd been given more details. But "first turning on the right" was clear enough.

"We take the smaller passage," he said as he approached the Horn People. Some of them gasped; Humphrey groaned. Simon looked sharply at him, but he showed no sign of making more trouble. "This has to be the way," Simon continued, trying to sound confident though he was aware that he hadn't looked it recently. "In fact we're lucky we didn't go the other way. I almost missed this one." No one rejoiced in their good fortune.

Certainly not Arnold. Simon happened to catch

that familiar expression of disgust, and it struck him funny. He grinned at Arnold, who merely looked away, but the grin did more for the Horn People than his words had. Some of them relaxed a little, and Sarah whispered something to The Row, whose expression brightened. She began to sing:

Row row row your bean
Slippery down the flume

The others joined:

Merrily merrily merrily merrily
Weave it on your loom

It wasn't exactly what he expected, from Sarah's version, but it made every bit as much sense, and it was just what was needed now. He waved Lightning once and started on his hands and knees into the tunnel. He could hear Joe's voice in song right behind him, and realized he'd forgotten about Humphrey. But it didn't matter now. Humphrey would have blocked the light in a space this small.

There was room enough to walk, bent at the waist, and Simon tried that, then hands and knees again, then walking with bent knees. Finally he settled on crawling. The Horn People would have an advantage over him here, where four legs were handier than two.

The tunnel began to get warm, and the air in it stuffy. Wherever it was going, it couldn't be open at the other end. Which could mean that they were where they should be. Before long there appeared another sign of that, though not one that Simon greeted happily. Swinging from side to side as he crawled, his shoulders began to touch the sides of the tunnel. It was one thing to think about a narrowing tunnel, and another to be inside one. This one he didn't like at all, and the difficulty in crawling increased as the tunnel began to climb slightly.

When the solid rock gave way to soil, Simon was glad that it was damp. At least there would be no dust. But the tunnel was narrowing more quickly now, and for the first time since he'd put on his suit, Simon found the horn a nuisance. It began to catch on the top of the tunnel, so he found it easier to look down than ahead. But then his back began to rub. And then, with breath becoming harder and harder to catch, he had to lie full length and push himself forward with knees and elbows. *We'd better get somewhere soon*, he thought, pushing down panic.

Inching forward with his whole body, he had a little more head room, but he didn't raise his eyes until he felt his shoulders begin to catch. This was something that hadn't occurred to him. What if he was in the right tunnel and couldn't reach the end of it? "Be there," he said under his breath, and looked up quickly. But it wasn't there. There was just more tunnel. He wriggled forward another four or five metres, as far as he could without the risk of getting stuck. His heart was pounding, his breath was coming fast, not only because the air seemed on the point of giving out.

It was a bad moment. He was exhausted, and near

to losing control, far from cool enough to remember that he could simply give the order to retreat down the tunnel. Instead, a thought leaped into his mind before he could check it. *We'll never get out of here! We're trapped!* A groan escaped him.

"Simon?" The voice was Joe's, and it brought Simon back to himself. He raised his head. Not all the way, because the horn struck the tunnel roof, but far enough so that, looking out of the tops of his eyes, he could see . . . was that wood ahead? "Simon!" It was a shout of terror, but Simon wanted to be sure what he was seeing before he answered. He took a hint from Humphrey and butted his horn at the tunnel above, soil falling on his head, and butted till he could see properly. And he saw what he wanted to see. There was a door. Still at least two metres away, but it was there, and Simon's self-control, his leadership, flowed back.

"Joe! Pass the word to back up."

"What, what?"

"No questions, Joe, please." He was panting with the exertion of talking. "We're nearly there, but I need some room to work. About three body-lengths." He lay with head in arms to gather his energy and wait until the word reached the end of the line. When it returned it was accompanied by a low moan which told him that he had to hurry. Some of the Horn People must be panicking. He inched back until Lightning was even with the farthest spot he'd reached, and began to chop and scrape at the sides of the tunnel, moving forward little by little into the widened space. It was hard, slow work, because he could get so little leverage, but he made steady progress. Not with speed enough to suit those behind him. The moan rose to a whine, and more voices took it up. *Where is The Row*, Simon thought, *with her song*? He hacked at the tunnel, hacked and chopped, his arms aching.

And finally he touched the door with the very point of Lightning. Then squeezed himself forward, pulled Lightning beneath him, the hilt as far as his chest. And shoved with both hands. Whunk! Nothing. He freed the point. Again, whunk! This time the door shuddered, and budged. *Once more now*. With all his strength. Whunk! And the door tipped outward. Only Lightning, lodged in it, held it back. Simon pulled sharply, and the door fell outward, landing with a crash. Sweet, fresh air rushed into the tunnel, and Simon filled his lungs gratefully. He gathered his strength and wriggled forward, more slowly than ever, it seemed, but with his heart rising. Now that they were all but out.

XIII

The Bridge, The Beast

The sky was blue and cloudless; the sun was a welcome warmth, even though he was hot from his exertions in the tunnel. The touch of a breeze on his face felt lovely. On the other hand, he was standing on a cliff-ledge, looking across a wide chasm at another cliff. It was disappointing not to see more of the route ahead, but there was no time to look about now, because only Joe had joined him on the ledge. What were the others doing? He looked into the tunnel and saw Humphrey–stuck. Well, not completely stuck, but barely moving. The bulk that made him a ferocious foe was no advantage in such a tight fit. A little annoyed that he wouldn't be the first to investigate the new situation, Simon crawled back into the tunnel he'd been so relieved to escape.

Humphrey's problem was not the width of the tunnel, but the depth. If he raised himself high enough on his feet to creep a little, his back caught. It clearly cost him great effort to move a centimetre, and he must have been straining as he was now for quite some distance. Simon hooked a foot on each side of the entrance, grabbed the base of Humphrey's horn, and pulled. Without much success, because Humphrey redoubled his efforts to push, and his feet actually acted as brakes. "Just lie flat, Humphrey," Simon directed. "Let me do the work." Humphrey needed no persuasion. He sagged. There was no moving that dead weight with ease, but Simon did manage, little by little, in short bursts of effort, to haul Humphrey along, sliding himself backwards, grasping the tunnel with his knees, then finally standing outside, bracing his feet for a last drag.

When Humphrey reached his feet on the ledge, he seemed nearly done in, but immediately took up his position opposite Simon and helped to direct the emerging Horn People, one right, one left along the ledge. It was good to see the desperation on their faces give way to excitement when they caught sight of the open air. It was best of all to see Sarah's relief.

Humphrey slumped where he stood, with his legs twitching in spasms.

"We made it, Humphrey," Simon said. "Good work." Humphrey mumbled in his exhaustion, but Simon caught part of it, ". . . welcome," and what was left of his hardness towards Humphrey melted away. He patted him, then stood up to survey the Horn People, strung out along the ledge in various positions of collapse. Humphrey had had by far the worst of it in the tunnel, but the strain had not all been physical. It would take them a few minutes to recover.

Except for Joe, now approaching from the left.

"I've been exploring, Simon Jesse."

"Good. What have you found?"

"It's *not* good. This is just a shelf we're on, and it stops."

"What, both ways?"

Joe nodded. "But there's this," he said importantly, and ducked behind Simon, who turned to see an iron stake driven into the ledge, with a thick rope looped over it. The rope crossed the gulf to a ledge on the cliff opposite, where another stake anchored it. Now that his attention was drawn there, Simon saw that steps had been hacked into a diagonal seam of rock leading to the top of the cliff.

"Are you sure there's no way out on this side? Let's have a look."

But Joe was right. In one direction the ledge narrowed till it disappeared into the sheer rock face. In the other it was merely interrupted, and continued, tantalizingly, about three metres away, but there was no way across the gap. Now Simon feared he knew what Arthur Toad had meant by the bridge. It hardly seemed the right word to describe a tightrope. And when the bridge came back to him, something else came with it: the beast below. Taking a deep breath and holding it, he leaned out and looked down, and Joe did likewise.

It was almost disappointing to see only rock rubble, a few boulders, at the bottom of the chasm. He released his breath. There were bones scattered about, as well, and a few nearly-whole animal skeletons. But no beast to be seen. Simon fought down his relief. Arthur Toad had been right about everything so far. Unless "below" referred to whatever was over the top of the cliff, past those steps. *Could be.*

Beside him, Joe suddenly stiffened, and the fur stood up along his back. He crept away from the edge.

"What is it, Joe," Simon whispered. No answer.

Simon looked into the chasm again, saw nothing, then dropped to hands and knees, inched closer to the edge, and looked directly down the face of the rock. His eyes scanned the bottom. And then he went cold. The beast was motionless, very like the rock in colour, so it didn't immediately stand out from its surroundings, and it was nothing like Simon could possibly have expected. At first he thought he was looking at some kind of serpent, but then he realized that the thing was a tail. It thickened at one end and joined a huge, scaly body. And the body joined a broad reptilian head with eye-bulges on either side. Part of one leg was visible, and its foot had ugly-looking claws in it. The thing was perfectly motionless. *Why is it so still*, Simon wondered when he had recovered a little from his shock. Surely it wouldn't have died standing up. *Too good to be true. Asleep?*

At least he'd seen the beast before it saw him, and that gave him time to think. Those whitened bones told him what it would mean to fall near the beast, though one might well not survive the fall. At the same time, the beast had no way of reaching the ledge or the rope. Simon moved to Joe, who was still trembling, and put a comforting hand on his back. A plan was forming. He waved Sarah over.

"There's a beast down there," he said quietly, and she made as if to look for herself.

"No, Sarah. Don't bother. Listen to what I'm

thinking. I'm pretty sure it doesn't know we're here. It's just standing there, and as long as it does that it's no problem. But we have to go across that rope.''

Sarah merely glanced at the bridge. "Can the beast reach it?'' she asked. The prospect of crossing the bridge didn't seem to alarm her in the least, and that gave Simon an idea. *If the rope isn't going to bother them, why not just send them over it?* The thought was tempting. *Freedom on the other side*, after all. Hadn't he already done what was expected of him, bringing the Horn People this far? *Very* tempting. What reason did he have to cross? Even as he asked himself the question, though, he realized that reasoning wouldn't help him to do what was right. With a sigh he returned his attention to Sarah, who was now looking at him inquiringly.

"No," he replied. "It couldn't get near us. But I think . . . Joe, can you keep quiet about the beast? What do you think, Sarah? It might be better if most of us have only the rope to think about as we cross."

"Won't the beast notice us?"

"Well, we'd be taking a chance, I suppose. It looks as if it's dozing or something. It's standing up, though."

"Let's try it. Should we tell The Row?"

"If you think so."

While Sarah fetched The Row, something else occurred to Simon. As they approached, he said, "Tell Humphrey too." Sarah looked at Humphrey, still where he'd collapsed, but now sitting up alertly, his eyes on them. When Sarah called, he got up obediently and joined them.

Simon quickly sketched the situation in for Humphrey and The Row.

"What do you say, The Row?" asked Sarah.

"I think Simon's right."

"Humphrey?" Humphrey was looking at the rope. There seemed to be something on his mind, but he said "I agree."

"Fine," said Simon. "Now you three tell the others. Tell them to be quiet, just to look at the rope when they cross." The Row and Sarah left, but Humphrey hesitated.

"Is everything clear, Humphrey?"

"Yes, yes, but . . ." Humphrey obviously had something to say that was hard to find words for. "But . . . Simon Jesse . . ." Simon began to sense what was coming.

"Go ahead, Humphrey."

"Well look, Simon Jesse . . ." Now the words unlocked, and came in a rush. "Listen, I feel stupid. I *am* stupid. You were right, and I was so stupid . . ." He shook his head. "Stupid. But listen, anything you want me to do. Do you want me to take on that beast?" He drew himself up and expanded his big chest. "Where is it, anyway?"

"No, Humphrey. I think the beast would be a bit much, even for you. All you can do now is tell the others about the rope. But Humphrey."

"Yes?"

"I'm glad you're . . . well, I'm glad."

"So am I, Simon Jesse, I really am."

"Okay then." And Humphrey hurried off.

"How about you, Joe? There's nothing to that

beast, really. We'll just scurry across over his head. He'll never even notice us. Right?''

"Right, Simon Jesse.'' But Joe's voice did not ring with confidence.

"So you're up to it?''

"I think so.''

"That's the way. You've been a big help, Joe, you and your eyes. A big help.'' That was obviously the best thing he could have said. Joe swelled with pride, and Simon decided he really would be all right.

He stood up and stepped to the rope. *One of us is not likely to scurry,* he thought.

XIV

The Rope

By foot or by hand? Simon considered the two possible ways to cross that bridge, while he pulled at it to make sure it was anchored securely on the other side. Both methods had drawbacks. If he tried walking over the rope, there was the chance of losing his balance. If he tried going hand over hand, beneath it, he couldn't be sure his arms would be strong enough to hang on.

The rope was tightly woven of several thick strands of fibre, and it was strung between the two stakes with a good deal of tension. It wasn't going to sway much. Simon sent his eyes across, metre by metre, preparing himself to walk it. He wished he'd had some practice at this sort of thing, though it occurred to him that a little practice might be worse than none if he found himself falling. That would hardly build confidence for the real thing.

Too much thinking. It could keep him off the rope entirely.

He tested the rope with one foot, trying to gauge how much it would give under his full weight. Then he put his whole mind into his feet, stepped onto the rope, felt his toes divide around it. He stepped back and turned one foot slightly outward so the rope crossed his arch diagonally when he slid his foot onto it again. He followed immediately with one step, another, going by feel, not looking at his feet but at a spot on the rope ahead, moving cautiously but smoothly, whispering "left foot, right foot" to himself. Concentrating on the rhythm, right foot, left, thinking so hard about it that he forgot about thinking. His lips still moved, left foot, right foot, but now his vision seemed to blur till he was seeing, right foot, not the rope but a picture, a picture of a boy not himself, left, a little older than him, but familiar-looking. On his hands and knees in the shade of a large maple tree, smiling at someone beside him. Right, left, the smile made Simon feel good. He felt he'd like to talk to that boy who looked–what did he look like? Left, right, the boy was up off his knees now, resting on his haunches, brushing his hands together, still smiling, left–the next step was on to the ledge, and the feel of solid rock underfoot banished the boy from his mind. Immediately he turned to check on the beast.

From his new vantage point, Simon could see that the beast's head was mostly jaw, resting on its breast, just above its smallish, limp-hanging front legs. But the important thing was that it hadn't moved. Simon waved his signal for the Horn People to come across.

Humphrey came first, Joe second. The Horn People poured across the rope in waves. One no sooner stepped off it than another stepped on. They scurried over so sure-footedly they might have done it every day of their lives. Still, Simon followed each of them with his eyes, saying to himself "Come on, that's right, that's right," as if he were thinking his friends across, keeping them steady with his mind. The number of Horn People on the far side lessened, lessened, until the last one, Sarah, stepped onto the rope and whisked over to him.

Since he had kept it to himself, the Horn People had no way of knowing what Simon knew–that they had just passed the last of the obstacles Arthur Toad had named. Simon sensed that they were all but home, and in his delight he made a mistake. He greeted Sarah with open arms.

"We made it, Sarah! We made it!"

"Yes, we made it," she answered, quickly picking up the jubilation in his voice. So did the others. A ragged cheer broke out, and began to swell through the ranks of the Horn People, many of whom could not have known exactly what they were cheering about.

Then a terrible roar split the air, and the cheering stopped as abruptly as if a door had been shut on it. The Horn People froze, exchanged frightened glances, then crowded cautiously forward to look into the chasm. Simon could not help but join them to look at the beast, fully roused now, baring a bank of long, pointed, yellowish teeth as he raged.

With a sinking heart, Simon recollected himself and rushed along the line of Horn People, urging them back, shushing those who had actually begun to taunt the beast. They obeyed him, but not without question. "Why, Simon Jesse?" one of them asked. "It can't get at us, can it?"

"Didn't you say we'd made it?" put in another. "The thing isn't dangerous now, is it?"

"Not to you, no," Simon said between his teeth, "not to you. But I have to go back."

There was a sudden pocket of shocked silence, before the news spread. "Has to go back," Simon heard repeated, and "No!" from several voices. One of them was Sarah's.

"No!" she said, rushing up to him, "no, Simon. You'll be staying with us." She was trying to sound confident, as if there could be no argument, but her tone betrayed her fears.

"I can't, Sarah. Wow, *lis*ten to that racket." The beast was screaming now, bellowing in what sounded like frustration as much as rage, and it almost seemed to be making words.

"SKOE! S-KOE! S-KOE!"

"Can you make that out?" Simon asked.

"No. Simon, you *must* stay."

"I get the feeling it isn't very happy. You know what it sounds like to me?"

"What?"

"It sounds like a great pair of lungs."

"Simon," Sarah said reproachfully, "this is not funny. You never said you were going to leave us. And how *can* you, now? How . . ."

"I have to go, Sarah. That comes from Arthur Toad, like everything else."

"But . . ."

"Sarah, at least let's get away from this noise. Let's get up those steps. We'll be able to talk better there."

"Well . . . maybe the beast will shut up. Maybe it'll forget it saw us."

"Yes, maybe."

There was no distinction between Humphrey's followers and those of Sarah–none that Simon could see as he watched them climb the steps. The Row and her singers were still in a group, though. They went up together. Finally only Humphrey and Simon were together on the ledge. Humphrey stood aside, but Simon motioned him ahead.

The steps were roughly cut into the rock. *The Mole People couldn't have made these*, Simon thought. To take his mind off the beast, still clamouring behind him, he counted as he climbed. *Twenty-three, twenty-four, twenty* . . . Humphrey had halted on the top step. "What . . ." Simon began, then noticed that Humphrey's attention was caught by something above him. Simon lifted his eyes to where a large bird was gliding effortlessly in the light wind. Still watching the bird, Simon nudged Humphrey, who stood aside to make room. Together they watched the bird beat its wings softly, bank and hover.

"Beautiful," Simon said.

"Wish I could do that." Humphrey sounded envious.

"Me too, Humphrey. I wouldn't have to walk back over that rope." So much for taking his mind off the beast.

There was no answer from Humphrey. Simon glanced at him and saw that his gaze was now fixed on something below him, something that had caused his lower jaw to drop.

XV

A New Home

How could they be up so high? The tunnels and chambers where Simon had met the Horn People would not have been anywhere near the centre of the earth, where the rock is so hot that it flows. The tunnels had been cool, even clammy. But now that he was looking down the side of a mountain, he had the odd impression that the Horn People had lived buried, for all those years, beneath miles and miles of rock. It couldn't have been so, or the way out would have been more of a climb than it was, but that was how it felt. It had been wonderful to break out of that last tunnel into the air, but there was no comparing that with this. The view was breathtaking. For the moment it completely lifted from Simon all thoughts of the beast, and of the return journey still to come.

After a bare patch of loose shale, interrupted by low outcroppings of the rock underneath, a few shrubs appeared, then a sprinkling of small trees quickly thickened and soon completely covered the side of the mountain. Lower down there were other trees, taller ones, in all sorts of shape and every shade of green. There must have been a spring somewhere in the trees, because here and there stretches of a stream stood out, and there was a glimpse of what looked like a waterfall. It was impossible to see where the stream joined the wide river that meandered through the valley between this mountain and the higher, green-carpeted one that rose across from it.

A shaggy animal with two curled horns emerged from behind a large rock on the right, not twenty metres away. Surprised by the crowd of silent watchers, it stopped, sized them up haughtily, as if to say "Who are you, and what are you doing on my mountain?" Then it vanished, breaking the spell of silence as it left.

Sarah detached herself from a knot of Horn People, as did The Row from her singers, and they approached Simon where he stood beside Humphrey. As at a signal, the rest of the Horn People turned and crowded up into an uneven semicircle. Simon felt a little like a king about to receive a deputation from some foreign power. Except that these people were his own. Almost his own. Something more than his appearance, something he didn't understand, was separating him from them. He felt his difference very keenly now, and sadly.

"Isn't this something, Sarah," he said. That didn't seem enough. He wanted to include them all. "Isn't it incredible?" This time his eyes swept over the whole group. There were murmurs of agreement, but they were quiet ones. The new home was obviously not the main thing on their minds just now.

"Simon," Sarah said, and the sad way she spoke his name showed that she had begun to face up to the inevitable parting. "Simon, is there anything I can do to persuade you?"

"No, Sarah. But look, all of you, you're home. You don't need me now." He was trying to turn aside sad thoughts with happy ones, but it couldn't be done.

"It's not a question of needing, Simon," said The Row. "We want you to stay."

A lump rose in his throat. He had to swallow several times before he could answer, and then his voice was husky.

"Yes, I know." He had to gulp again. "I'm sorry I have to leave. I told Sarah that Arthur Toad said I have to go back, but it's not only that. I feel . . . I know I have to." He paused, unable to find words to say how that tower called him. To his past and his future, still as much a riddle as ever, but there was just one way to solve it. "You know," he said, addressing everyone, "we should really feel wonderful. In fact I do, in a way. It wasn't easy, what we did, but here we are. Here we are," he repeated, rather lamely. He wasn't making anyone feel better, least of all himself. But he could see that the Horn People were through resisting. "I have to go now," he finished.

"We'll come down and see you off, then," said Sarah.

Simon looked once more down the mountain, turned and briefly grasped the base of Humphrey's horn, hard. Then he started down the steps.

Part Four

THE RETURN

XVI

Brave Simon Jesse

What was the beast doing, now that it was quiet again? Simon resisted the temptation to look. Instead, he surveyed the rope, trying to convince himself that it was his only problem, that nothing significant had changed when the beast awakened. *Things are no different now.* His mind agreed, but his body didn't seem so sure. His legs felt heavy.

When he turned to say good-bye, he found all of the Horn People descending the steps. Sarah noticed his surprise.

"Don't worry," she said, "they won't make any noise."

"I wasn't worried. I just didn't expect . . ."

"We all want to say good-bye, Simon. You're very dear to us all, you know."

The tears that Simon had so far managed to hold back now began to flow, and he could only let them come. He didn't try to hide them as he passed along the line of Horn People, taking leave of each one. Arnold was near the end of the line, and it was not lost on Simon that he must have been among the first down the steps. Now he was sitting stiffly on his haunches, staring straight ahead, as though he were still on duty, still guarding some imaginary portcullis. Simon responded to the sight much as he had back at the cavern, but this time his amusement was very much mixed with affection. If any of the others had looked the way Arnold did now, one could only have concluded that they were not in the least moved by this parting. But for Arnold to have traded his normal expression of disgust for no expression at all–that was a big change. Simon noted it, pleased, and passed on.

He gave Joe an extra pat on the way back to where Sarah, Humphrey and The Row stood together. He knelt and gave them each a hug. He held on to Sarah for a long time, wordlessly. Then he turned to the rope.

As before, he gave himself no time to build up any resistance, though he braced himself for the reaction of the beast to his appearance. Perhaps that was what made him start too quickly. He knew, before he had taken three steps, that his rhythm was wrong, too jerky, and that he was lingering too long between steps. He made an effort to adjust, and it was then that the beast caught sight of him. He couldn't help starting at the bellow that erupted from below, even though it was expected. His foot met the rope just a little too squarely, and he had to follow with a quick step to compensate. It spoiled his delicate balance and stopped him, his arms thrashing the air in an attempt to regain it.

"Simon!" Sarah's cry rang out. He made a feeble attempt to signal with his hand, don't worry, but it was lost in the windmilling of his arms. For an agonizing moment not only his arms, but his hips, shifted from side to side as he stood on the now-vibrating rope. Then his body jack-knifed and he lost his balance completely. He was on the point of toppling when some instinct made him step off the rope with one foot, catch at it with the other knee and both hands. He dangled that way till the knee slipped off and he ended with a wrenching drop to arm's length, facing the way he'd come. There he hung, aware of the Horn People on the rock just above his line of vision. Their cries of alarm and encouragement, and the roar of the beast, seemed to come from a great distance.

He managed the difficult manoeuvre of turning under the rope, then pulled himself up a little to take the strain off his shoulder blades, before he began advancing, painfully, hand over hand. A little beyond half way his fingers began to feel numb, and he made another effort to haul himself up. He had an idea he might be able to hook an elbow over the rope for a rest, maybe even balance on his chest for a bit. But he hadn't the strength to get high enough, and the effort was wasted.

Hanging at full length again, he became aware of the voices of the Horn People behind him. He recognized the tune of Row Row Row, sung as slowly and mournfully as a dirge. He placed one hand in front of the other. Either his whole body pulsed with the effort, or the song swelled, or both. The other hand, now, and again the swelling of voices. And he began to accept the rhythm of the song, tried to match it, hand over hand over hand. To the ledge, whereupon the song burst into a rollicking tempo, a celebration.

One hand on the rope, the other on the ledge, he felt without success for footing on the side of the cliff. Nothing to do but scrabble with his feet at nonexistent steps, and lift, lift, an elbow onto the rope, then a leg, then grab at the iron stake, drag himself onto the cliff. He rolled away from the edge to lie, eyes closed, exhausted. He scarcely heard the wild cheering across the way.

But he did hear a new song begin, tentatively at first, then more surely. He sat up to listen, and found himself hearing what he never expected to hear. It fulfilled a prediction of Arthur Toad that he had entirely forgotten.

Buried with our fears
   Brave Simon Jesse
Living with our tears
   Brave Simon Jesse

One hundred years have passed
   Brave Simon Jesse
You came to us at last
   Brave Simon Jesse

Leader through the dark
   Brave Simon Jesse
All the People hark
   To brave Simon Jesse

Walker on the rope
   Brave Simon Jesse

Maker of our hope
  Brave Simon Jesse

Lightning in your hand
  Brave Simon Jesse
You led us to our land
  Brave Simon Jesse

People of the Horn
  Brave Simon Jesse
Glad that you were born
  Brave Simon Jesse

The song ended in cheers and shouts of farewell.
Simon stood up and waved both hands to show his
appreciation, too full of emotion and a strange embarrassment to do more. He watched the Horn People
file up the steps. He saw each of them outlined against
the waning light of the sky, before they disappeared.
Finally he was alone, except for the beast who had
kept up his wild accompaniment to the song of the
Horn People, and now carried on by itself.

Perhaps it was his own sudden loneliness, but Simon fancied he heard a note of desolation in the
beast's unintelligible tirade. He had a brief vision of
the beast as a trapped and lonely creature, condemned
to kill and eat anyone who, literally, dropped in to
visit. That and the dying of the light made him shiver.
It struck him as rather odd, as he drew Lightning,
that he'd never once thought of the sun on the way
out. Now he knew he was going to miss it, and the
idea of being alone in double darkness gave the return
journey a certain aura of menace.

XVII
Lightning

Simon reached his feet in the cavern, after a hateful time on hands and knees in the tunnel, which seemed still to echo with the desperate cries of the Horn People. But the perfect silence of the cavern was worse, more eerie than ever. Shining Lightning into the emptiness, as he had before, Simon wondered what was making this place feel so different. The absence of the Horn People, he supposed. He sidled towards the tunnel that issued from it, reluctant to turn his back. Reaching the entrance, he turned into it and ran. For about twenty-five metres.

Two ugly insects, taller than Humphrey, stood abreast in the tunnel, and there were others behind them.

"Yah!" taunted one of them, with a rusty-sounding voice. "Smell you."

"Smell you blood," the other added, and their claws, at least a half metre long, clacked as they opened and closed. Keeping his eyes on the advancing insects, fighting down nausea, Simon backed up. Only the two followed him, though the others clacked their support.

"Blood," said the first, chillingly.

"Where go?" said the other. "Where you go, stink?"

"Smell you," repeated the first. "Kill you now."

It wasn't clear whether these creatures were stupid, or just struggling with an unfamiliar language, but they certainly looked equipped for what they were proposing to do, scuttling forward on stick legs, their bulging eyes glittering on each side of armoured, hatchet-shaped heads. Simon turned and fled the way he had come. He gained the cavern entrance just as two more of the creatures appeared in it. A trap!

There was no time to think, but there was nothing to think about. There was nothing to do but fight. Simon skidded to a stop and hacked wildly at one of the newcomers, missing entirely, distracted by the sight of others thronging up behind these two. He chopped again, and Lightning clanged on the side of the tunnel. He gathered himself, took aim and severed the neck of one of the creatures. That settled him down a little. These things were not invulnerable, at least. But there was no time to waste, with the others behind him. He slashed at the second insect, disabled it, stepped past it and fought his way back into the cavern, where he stood with his back to the wall.

He had not been wrong to feel a difference in the cavern. It was alive with the huge insects, who must have been waiting, just out of sight, till he left it. Now the monsters crowded around him. "Blood!" they cried, "Smell you," and "Kill!" Simon flashed Lightning around in a semicircle, keeping them at bay for the moment. He had a strong impulse to leap into the tunnel to the outside world, but what would that accomplish? He knew only one way to the tower—past these terrible creatures, now or later. It might as well be now, if it was possible at all.

"Kill my brother, stink," said one of the two insects now appearing from the tunnel.

"Kill you now," the other said, and feinted an attack. Simon reacted, but not as expected. He met the creature head-on with a lunge that missed, but then he sheared its head off with his recoil. As he did so, he felt a claw close on his leg, chopped down at it, kicked himself free, laid fiercely about him with Lightning. The creatures had closed in swiftly and now found themselves too near the bite of the sword. Simon hacked and hacked, aiming for necks when he could penetrate the guard of the pincers, slashing off legs, chopping bodies which soon piled up before him. He had a breather, then, while insects in the second rank began to pull at the mass of carcasses, apparently to clear the way for another assault.

No more of the insects from the tunnel had appeared, though that was little relief. The creatures he could see greatly outnumbered him already, and there was no way to tell how many more were lurking in the darkness. What to do? *Am I going to have to kill them all to get out of here?* He considered the possibility without fear, aroused by his taste of fighting, and his success. But he wasn't underestimating the challenge before him. Suddenly he went on the offensive, chopping over the dead and wounded bodies at those engaged in removing them. That caused a general retreat.

A voice came out of the gloom. "Not fair! Kill my brother!"

"Not fair!" Simon couldn't believe his ears. He might have beem amused if he weren't so angry. "This wasn't my idea," he said. "I'll kill the rest of your brothers if I have to.

"Now come on! Come on, you uglies. Come and meet *my* brother." Lightning whistled through the air. No one accepted the invitation.

Simon's position was stronger than it had been. He'd killed or seriously wounded more than a dozen of the insects and was himself unharmed. He decided to use the present impasse to bargain.

"Who's your leader?" he asked of the insects at large. No answer. He repeated the question.

"Kill my brother," was the morose reply.

"You mean he's dead?"

Nothing.

"Listen, you call the others. You call your brothers out of that tunnel." He gestured towards it with Lightning. "Call them in here. You understand?" There was no response other than the hollow clicking of claws. "Call your brothers. I no kill."

"Stink!"

"All right, then." *Stupid things*. "You'll be sorry." Simon kicked aside a couple of bodies, moved to the opening of the tunnel, quickly looked into it. No sign of the others. Were they under orders to stay where they were? Too stupid to join the fight? Stupid. The word made him think of Humphrey, how he'd have liked a chance at these creatures. Compared with them, Humphrey was brainy. There was no talking to them at all, even though he'd fought them to a standstill. The next move seemed to be up to him.

So he moved. He vaulted the bodies in front of him and attacked the nearest insects, decapitating two of them, crippling another. The remainder crowded in confusion to the far side of the cavern. He leaped here and there after them, disposing of three more before the rest disappeared into various openings. Then he raced back to the tunnel, now clearly marked by the bodies lying near it, rushed up to the front ranks of the insects in it. The first two reared to meet him, apparently taken aback. He killed one of them, shouting "Yah!" as he thrust, "kill your brother!" Immediately he hurried back to the cavern, to the centre of it, caught and dispatched another insect unprepared for his return. Others, just beginning to emerge from their holes, shrank back.

He leapt to where he'd first taken his stand, and sheathed Lightning, hoping that his foray into the tunnel would have the effect he wanted–to draw the insects from there into the cavern. He didn't want to find himself caught between the two forces, not again.

For a short time the silence was as perfect as the darkness, as Simon stood trying to control his breathing. He had a surprise in mind for the insects. He could see nothing at all, and he felt securely invisible. Had he been dealing with creatures more like himself, his plan would have been a good one. It had one flaw. He had not considered how the insects managed in the dark, though the evidence of their keen sense of smell was there in some of the things they had said.

A rustling. Rustling noises now, and minute dragging sounds. They seemed to come from everywhere. His flesh crept as he imagined insects pouring into the cavern in the dark. But still he waited. He wanted them all accounted for, if possible, confident now that their numbers were no match for Lightning.

Those dry scraping sounds. Getting closer? Or were they louder because the number of insects was growing? Perhaps the sounds were multiplied by his imagination. To force himself to stay invisible just a little longer, he counted to fifty, speeding up as he went. Then he drew Lightning. A moment longer and he would never have seen the plight he was in.

He was nearly surrounded by insects, so close the many facets of their eyes seemed to burn at him, and he could see each serration of their claws, each waving hairy pair of antennae. He screamed with fright, just as one of the creatures struck his left arm, this time with a numbing grip. There was nothing he could do about that, not now. He struck wildly at the others, feeling a pincer grab his leg and pull. He nearly lost his balance. He knew he would be lost if he went down. He hacked the insect at his leg, freed it, then tried to leap sideways to avoid another thrust. The creature gripping his arm was dragged heavily towards him, its other claw narrowly slashing past his head. Horribly, he felt its armoured body drawn close to his own. He drew Lightning back and stabbed. The insect sagged, its pincer still clamped to Simon's arm. Quickly he chopped it off, staggering back as the weight, but not the claw, dropped away. Now he was free to hack and hack at the insects thronging close. He laid about him with a strength born of fear, edging steadily to his left, stepping on and over the bodies that piled up before him, twice nearly slipping on some smooth surface. Finally he reached the entrance to the tunnel, still, or again, empty of insects. With his back to it, he aimed a flurry of slashes at the still-closing attackers. Then he turned and ran for all he was worth. He was determined to cut through anything in his way, rather than face another siege in the cavern.

But he reached the spot where he'd first met the insects and they were gone. He rushed on, praying that they had all been decoyed into the cavern. He ran just short of top speed, because he could see only so far ahead, and because he had to hold himself ready to stop and fight, if necessary. He ran and ran, bearing always to the left. When his feet encountered dust he knew he had not much farther to go, but he could see that many insect tracks had erased those of the Horn People. So the things had been this far. He could only hope they weren't here now. He sped recklessly on. And there was the light of the antechamber ahead. Nothing between him and it.

He flew into the antechamber, Lightning at the ready. But it was empty. He tossed Lightning down and heaved the door to. It closed with a thump, and he stood leaning against it, panting heavily. He had no idea how quickly the insects could move, or whether they would even have troubled to follow. Maybe they'd had enough. He'd given them plenty. But he was still full of the horror of the battle, and he still had a vivid reminder of it clamped to his arm. He tried to pull it off and winced as he realized that the skin of his arm was broken under a rip in the fur of his suit. He recovered Lightning, slid it between his arm and the spot where the jaws of the pincer met, and pried it open. It fell to the floor with a clatter.

Not much blood, but the arm felt terribly sore. He flexed and twisted it. Nothing broken, anyway. And he could hear nothing on the other side of the door. Maybe sound would not penetrate that thickness. If the insects had followed him, would they be able to push it open? He waited, his ears straining.

XVIII

The Tower

The longer he listened, in the quiet and light of the antechamber, the more he was persuaded that even creatures as beastly stupid as those insects would know when they were beaten. The surer he became that he was safe, the more his body relaxed. Before he knew it, his legs were trembling uncontrollably. He had to sit down on the bottom step of the tower. Soon he was shaking all over. Something was happening inside him too, and he found out what it was when it burst from him as a sob. Then he was weeping with great, racking convulsions. He was weeping away the pressure of terror that had built up inside him, releasing his revulsion for the insects and the slaughter they'd pushed him to, unnecessary slaughter. His only offence, so far as he knew, was trespassing. What was that, to provoke such savagery? His escape from it had been very narrow. He sobbed that out too.

His head resting on his arms atop his drawn-up knees, he cried till his body was drained of tension, his mind of its fears. When he was cried out he sighed deeply and straightened his back. Then he snickered.

Then he barked a laugh, "Ha!" If there had been

anything funny about the escape from the insects he might have released the pressure as thoroughly with hysterical laughter as he had with weeping. He had no energy left for another fit of emotion, but he'd been struck by the spectacle of a hero, himself, crying his guts out. "Brave Simon Jesse," he said aloud, and giggled. Arthur Toad had said something about the fears of heroes, but Simon had forgotten that.

The tower drew him strongly now, and yet he was reluctant to move. It wasn't his tiredness that kept him from stirring, though he was very tired, and sore. His arms and legs felt bruised. Apparently he'd taken more blows in the battle than he'd realized. But what fixed him where he sat was his mind, floating free of his body to thoughts of the journey. He could afford to do that, now that it was over–all but finished for him. He relived his mistakes. He burned with embarrassment over his clumsiness on the rope, never thinking of the grit that had gotten him across it. He shook his head at the foolishness of believing himself invisible in the cavern. His stratagem had worked, but it had very nearly been fatal.

The satisfaction he felt was for the Horn People. They had been spared the worst of the trip, bad though that last tunnel had been, and their new home was so lovely. He remembered it with pleasure, thinking of the fun of exploration it offered. He wondered what his friends were doing while he sat thinking of them.

His warmest thoughts, and his saddest ones, were of Sarah. In the short time they had spent together he had learned to admire her, and to love her. He missed Humphrey too, and Joe, and The Row. Even Arnold now seemed a sort who could be almost likeable, if you didn't expect too much of him. And there were many others whose names he hadn't even learned. He wished there had been time to get to know them all.

But always his thoughts returned with awe to the mystery of Arthur Toad. Arthur Toad had known everything before it happened, everything. He had foreseen the fate of the Horn People if they refused to flee their old burrows, he had predicted Simon's arrival, and he had been right about the journey. Thinking over his experiences, Simon realized how terrified he would have been to know all about them in advance. So that must have been part of Arthur Toad's wisdom too—telling him only what he needed to know and letting him find out for himself what it would involve. Looking back on it all, Simon approached a thought that was too immense to hold on to—what a terrible weight it would be, seeing things before they happened and having to leave the doing of them, well or badly, to others. In any case, he had no chance to pursue the thought, because a voice spoke without warning and scared him silly.

"How's she goin', Si?"

His reverie shattered, Simon leapt to his feet, blood rushing to his head, before he recognized the voice and recalled with some sympathy what Arnold had said about G.H.'s unannounced appearances.

"Oh, G.H. Phew! You scared me."

"Yeah? So how's things?"

"I'm fine, G.H."

"On yer way back now?"

"Yes."

"Well you hang loose, hear?"

"I hear. And I won't take any wooden watchama-callits."

"Attaboy." And G.H. flapped off into the Midnight Lake tunnel.

Simon stood still for a few moments. He half expected a last message from Arthur Toad, but nothing came. Finally he sighed and turned to look up the tower. A thought hit him. What about Lightning? And his suit? Was he to keep them? He walked to the mouth of the Midnight Lake tunnel and shouted.

"G.H.!"

When the echo died, he shouted again. There was no answer. He pondered, rubbing the fur of his right arm. His left was stiffening up. Then he unbuckled his belt and stood the scabbard against the wall as he stepped out of his suit. He carefully folded the bottoms, then the jacket, shivering slightly, and replaced them in the fur bag. Then the horn helmet.

Lightning. He picked up the sword, his lantern and his weapon, and looked it over lovingly. He cut at the air with it a few times, and had a moment's fierce satisfaction, recalling his battle with the insects. Then he sheathed it. The bag went in the hole under the flagstone, but there was no room for anything else. *I should really give Lightning back to Deep Well*, he thought, but the tower was beckoning urgently now. He compromised by placing Lightning in its scabbard on top of the replaced flagstone, wondering who else might ever find it there.

Simon felt all the muscles of his body resisting as he began to make his way up those spiral steps, around and up, as the light grew steadily dimmer. Each time he looked down, the circle of light below him was smaller, smaller. It shrank to a point, disappeared. He climbed by feel now, sliding his hand along the stone wall to make sure he kept away from the edge of the steps. He had no idea where the climb was taking him, but he grew more and more breathless with the exertion and the mounting excitement of realizing that he was getting close to finding out what Arthur Toad had meant by his greatest strength. Any moment now, something was going to . . .

XIX

Past and Future

Ping! *What*? Ping! Then a series of small, diminishing pings that sounded the way a flat stone looks when it's skipped on a lake. And the darkness was white. White, but not clear. It was thickly white, like milk, but he could breathe in it easily. He seemed to be half-walking, half-swimming in slow motion. Gliding gracefully, noiselessly. He closed his eyes to savour the feeling of near-weightlessness. Something touched his hand, lightly, and he opened his eyes to look at it. It was a plastic boat, floating in the liquid air. Now something was stirring the air. It swirled like a thick fog in a light wind. He could hear something too, what was it, distant voices? Laughter? And the air was warming up . . . He gave the boat a shove and it floated away from him till it hit the side of . . . The milky fog gathered in a vortex to one spot in the air above the tub. Quick as thought the vortex shrank and vanished.

"Simon!" His father's voice reached him.

"Simon. Si." That was Toby, giggling.

"Hey, Simon, did you hear me?"

He did and he didn't, because of that puzzling little whirlpool in the air—in his mind now, actually, and strangely hard to push out. He made an effort.

"Hm?"

His father chuckled. "What did I say?"

"About what?"

"Silly. Wash your face. And don't forget your neck. Toby's almost done."

Simon picked up the soap. The whirlpool was gone, but he didn't miss it. He was looking forward to talking with Toby about the toads.